TALON REPRISAL

TALON
BOOK 4

BRENT TOWNS

ROUGH
EDGES
PRESS

Talon Reprisal
Paperback Edition
Copyright © 2023 Brent Towns

Rough Edges Press
An Imprint of Wolfpack Publishing
9850 S. Maryland Parkway, Suite A-5 #323
Las Vegas, Nevada 89183

roughedgespress.com

Paperback ISBN 978-1-68549-229-8
eBook ISBN 978-1-68549-228-1
LCCN 2022951534

TALON REPRISAL

PREVIOUSLY...

Hereford, England

"TAKE A SEAT," Anja said, pointing at a chair.

Federov grinned. "We are all together again so soon. Did you have success with your mission?"

"We did, in fact."

"Good. I am pleased."

Hawk moved around behind him and suddenly the Russian became nervous. "Do you need another name from me? Is that it?"

Anja shrugged and looked at Hawk.

Suddenly Federov's face was traveling at speed towards the stainless-steel table he was seated at. There was a sickening sound as his nose flattened against the hard surface. Blood spurted and flowed onto the tabletop.

Hawk pulled the Russian's head back by his hair and said harshly into the stunned man's ear, "We know everything, bloke. You're the gaffer of the whole shithouse situation. The boss of it all. You had Noskov kill Medvedev and then used him as your proxy. But he was fucking up too much and you needed him gone before word got out."

1

"I don't know what—what you are talking about," Federov moaned.

"You screwed up, Leonid," Anja said. "The ship that Noskov was on was owned by you. Viktor wouldn't have made that mistake. Then, when we took Noskov alive, he confirmed everything."

"Viktor left me behind. He cared about no one but himself." The bitterness and bile flowed out of the Russian. "But he underestimated me and my will to get revenge."

Anja nodded. "You played your part well. Giving us information which we could prove while you connived in your cell. I'm still at a loss how you did the rest of it but I'm sure it will all come out."

Hawk moved back around to Anja's side. He said, "But now your time with us is at an end. We're handing you over to MI5. From here on out you'll be their problem."

Federov looked up at them, his face bloody. His eyes narrowed. "You will hear of me again. I will not go quietly into the night. Do not make the same mistake Viktor made."

Hawk's voice grew savage. "I'd like to kill you, asshole, but they won't let me. Keep it up and I might just do it anyway."

Federov spat. "Go ahead, do it."

Hawk took a step toward him. "Jake, stop."

He froze, staring at the Russian with hatred. "You're lucky she's here, mate."

"You will never succeed," Federov snapped.

"We already have," said Anja. "Through that one slipup you made with the ship, we've managed to find all of Medusa's foreign bank accounts. Everything has been frozen. Right now, SAS teams along with partner forces are hitting targets across the globe, freeing women you have as captives ready to sell. They are also seizing weapons shipments. Medusa is done, Leonid. You are now boss of nothing. You thought Noskov was endangering everything, but you were the one who brought it down."

Hawk grinned. "Oops."

Federov sat there in silence, eyes darting left and right as he processed what he'd just been told. Then realization hit. It was all over. The once great criminal empire was no more. Everything would fracture and he'd be stuck in some dark hole that MI5 put him in.

By the time Anja and Hawk left the room, he was wailing like a spoilt child.

———

THEY ALL SAT around the table drinking beer. Tomorrow they would attend the memorial of a friend. The forecast was for rain, weather which would be suitable for such a solemn occasion.

Hawk looked across the table at Slania. He pointed his bottle at her and said, "You did good, lass."

"I'm glad you approve." He wasn't sure if there was sarcasm there or not, but took it good naturedly.

Anja said, "Yes, I think you will fit right in. That is if you want to stay."

Slania nodded. "I'll stay."

"Mister Gray?"

"You'll not be able to shake me loose, Boss. But there is one thing."

"What is that?"

"Who do I see about those suits? They work, but it bloody hurts when you get shot."

They all chuckled.

Anja's cell rang and she got up and moved away to answer it. Ilse was sitting next to Hawk, and he felt her hand cover his under the table. He opened his to accept it

3

and glanced at her. She smiled. "Now that Medusa is gone, what shall we do?"

"There will be fractures in the underworld that will need healing in our own special way," Hawk replied.

Slania said, "I heard that the cleanup teams have freed over four-hundred sex slaves across Europe."

Ilse nodded. "Yes, but there will be those who slip through the cracks."

"We'll never be out of a job," Hawk said.

Anja disconnected the call, a look of concern on her face. "What's up, Boss?" Gray asked.

"Leonid Federov was found dead in his cell twenty minutes ago."

"That'll stuff up your day," Hawk said.

"That isn't all," Anja continued, staring at the former SAS operator. "In the words of someone famous, whose porridge did you piss in?"

Hawk frowned. "Why?"

"Someone has just put a twenty-million-dollar bounty on your head. You're now a wanted man, Jake."

CHAPTER ONE

Naples, Italy

"DAMN IT, how many times do you have to be told, don't steal the expensive vehicles?"

"Who said it was expensive?"

"It's a Maserati, Jake."

"That won't be a concern for very much longer because I'll be bloody dead," Jacob Hawk growled back at his boss over the comms. "Whoever made these streets so narrow needs poking in the eye with a forked stick."

Hawk stared at the armored SUV coming towards him, the light from the streetlamps flashing off the windshield as it sped by them. He saw the passenger lean out the window and open fire.

Bullets hammered into the luxury vehicle, making the 6-foot-4 former SAS operator with dark hair curse loudly. "Bastards."

"What's going on, Jake?" Anja Meyer asked in his earpiece.

"They're shooting at—" Hawk's retort was cut short as he took evasive action, swerving the Maserati into a series

5

of vacant car parks, utilizing the sidewalk where necessary to avoid the oncoming SUV. "Oh fucking hell."

The mirror on the passenger side disintegrated as it clipped the front of a stone-fronted building, spraying debris across the roof of the vehicle.

"Talk to me, Jake. What's happening?" Anja asked.

He dropped the Maserati back a gear and booted it. "We're all good, Boss. Not too much damage."

He could envisage her shaking her head, her short blonde hair flicking around her thin face. Dressing mostly in jeans, she was athletic and in her mid-thirties. Her second in command, Ilse Geller, would be beside her monitoring events, working scenarios on the run.

Ilse had mousy colored hair and fine features. Her athletic build was similar to Anja's. She was also proficient at her job as the team's intelligence officer, a role she had once filled when working with Anja for German Intelligence.

Then there was Gray. "Where the hell is Marcus?" Hawk snarled as he trod hard on the brake and turned the Maserati to the left down another narrow, cobbled street.

"He's closing in from your west," Ilse said. "Just keep moving in the direction you are now."

"What the hell happened to him?" Hawk asked.

"You stole a fast car, you bloody cock," a new voice said over the comms. "You expect me to keep up with you driving that, and me in a frigging clapped out van."

"There's nothing wrong with the van, Marcus," Anja said firmly. "It was purchased by me with company money."

"Say no more," said Hawk, rolling his eyes.

"Let's just concentrate on what we're doing, shall we?" the Talon commander said curtly.

"Jake, you've got two more vehicles coming at you from the east," Ilse cut in, issuing the warning in a matter-of-fact tone.

Hawk looked at the Neoclassical architectural buildings rising three floors on either side of the street lit with orange light and said, "What would you like me to do about it?"

"Tone, Jake."

"Why is it that you lot always remind me about my —Fuck!"

He jerked suddenly on the Maserati's wheel to avoid the two black SUVs coming at him from the right. Bullets sprayed the back of the luxury vehicle and the rear window shattered like confetti thrown at a wedding.

"What was that, Jake?" Anja asked.

"Rear window."

"Please tell me our package is still alive."

Hawk glanced over his shoulder at the form curled up in the rear seat. "Hey, Marco, you still alive?"

"Fuck you, British pig. My people will kill you fucking dead."

"Yes, he's still alive—"

More bullets punched into the rear of the Maserati and Hawk heard Marco grunt. He glanced back again and saw the Italian people smuggler hunched over to the side. "Oops."

"Give me fucking strength...you've just killed the only lead to whoever put the bounty on your head," he heard Anja mutter into her comms. "Ditch the million-dollar car, Jake, and get the hell out of there."

"Anything you say, Boss. Ilse, direct me to a rendezvous point with our tardy friend."

"Turn right at the next intersection."

"Roger."

He slowed ever so slightly and turned right as directed. Behind him were the three SUVs that were chasing him—the two new arrivals and the other one. "Marcus, can you hear me?"

"Like a drum in an elevator, old mate."

"Get ready to switch over."

"What?"

"Get ready to switch into the Maserati."

"What the hell, Jake?"

"You don't seriously expect us to outrun those assholes in the POS van, do you?"

"POS? What's POS?"

"Piece of shit."

"Point taken."

"Do not abandon the van, Jake," Anja ordered firmly.

"Sorry, Boss, you're breaking up."

Suddenly the comms came alive with every German expletive Anja could muster. There was not much that Hawk could do but reply, "Bless you."

———

HE COULD SEE the headlines now. *Shootout on Naples Street!* they screamed. Bullets punched into the van as Gray leaned back into cover to reload the Heckler and Koch 416. He dropped out the empty magazine and said through the bandana covering half of his face, "So much for a quick change over."

Hawk looked at the burning Maserati, acrid black smoke rising into the air. "The plan was sound, cock."

Gray rolled his eyes. "Yeah, mate, real fucking sound." He leaned out and fired at a shooter who was trying to flank them. "Fucking wanker."

The man went down in a heap and never moved.

Marcus Gray was a former Para from the Regiment and had five years' experience in various combat zones. Although in his late twenties, he appeared to be nineteen, his hair thick and dark. He was also extremely good at what he did.

Hawk said into his comms, "Alpha Two, we sure could use some assistance at this time."

"Bravo One, your exfil is to your east, over," Ilse said.

"Copy."

Hawk slid the door of the van open, reaching for his body armor. As he slipped into it, he did a quick but thorough check to ensure he had everything required. Then he grabbed Gray's. "Marcus."

"What?"

"Here."

The former Para turned. Hawk tossed him his kit. "Get into that before someone gets lucky. We're getting out of here." Hawk turned and covered him while he slipped into the body armor.

Gray said over the gunfire, "The boss seems quiet."

"She's pissed with me."

Gray glanced at the pyre. "Yep, I can understand that. Situation normal."

"You ready to move?" Hawk asked, firing at another shooter.

"When you are."

"Cover me."

Hawk broke clear of the van and sprinted towards an alley to their east. Behind him he could hear Gray methodically firing his weapon, careful not to waste too much ammunition and empty his magazine before Hawk had reached cover.

Once he was safe in the alley, Hawk took up a position where he could in turn cover Gray. "Ready when you are, Marcus."

As they say in the classics, head down ass up, Gray ran as fast as he could towards the alley. Hawk opened fire and managed to keep the Italian shooters pinned down.

The former Para was sucking in lungfuls of air when he reached Hawk's position. Hawk grinned as he said, "Bit out of shape, old boy?"

"Still run your ragged ass into the ground, mate."

"Fuck off. You shithead Paras couldn't run rings around a frigging turtle."

"Are you two done?" Ilse asked, butting in on the banter.

"Sure."

"Then get down to the end of the alley and turn left. Move."

They turned and ran once more. When they reached the end of the alley, they made the suggested turn and then moved further along the street. Behind them they could hear the Italians coming in their vehicles. Hawk glanced at Gray. "We're not going to outrun those scousers without wheels."

"No."

"I guess there's only one thing for it."

"I guess so," Gray agreed as they slowed to a walk.

"Bravo, what are you doing?" Ilse asked.

"Ever heard of the Alamo?" Hawk asked.

"Everyone died at the Alamo, Jake," Ilse said.

"Yeah, well, I'm not running anymore. Time to act like Custer."

"Your analogies aren't filling me with confidence, Bravo One."

He did a tactical reload and readied himself for what was to come. "Time to put on our big-boy pants, Marcus, and go to work."

"Isn't that the truth."

———

"SLANIA, WHERE ARE YOU?" Anja asked.

"I'm about five mikes out," she answered, her accent coming through.

Slania Albring was former Special Forces Group out of Belgium. After three years of service, she'd been plucked from SFG to go into intelligence. Right up until she was wanted by Interpol. Now, however, she worked for Talon.

Her physique was thin but hard muscled, and her hair was long and dark. What made her stand out was the myriad tattoos covering her body.

She was Talon's computer tech, but her special skills meant she could double in the field when required. This was one such time.

Anja looked at Ilse. "Get ready to evacuate. I want nothing left that suggests we were even here. I'll take comms while you do it."

"Yes, ma'am."

"Bravo One, copy?"

"Roger, Alpha One."

"Alpha Three is five mikes out and should be able to evacuate you," the Talon commander said.

"Sure thing, Boss. Is she up on comms?"

"I'm here, Jacob."

"There she is. Be aware that when you get here this place will be a shitstorm."

"My kind of weather," Slania replied. "I'm four mikes out and coming in hot."

Anja studied the screen before her, each flashing dot one of her team. Her gaze went to the three squares closing in on Hawk and Gray. "Jake, you're about to have company."

"We'll welcome them with open arms, ma'am, as long as they wipe their boots."

———

HAWK GRABBED the fragmentation grenade from his webbing and waited. Beside him, Gray said, "You just going to stand in the middle of the street and wait?"

"Maybe."

"No wonder you walk bow-legged."

11

Sudden gunfire erupted and bullets cut the air around the former SAS operator. Some ricocheted off the street with angry whines. Casually, as though he had no care in the world, Hawk pulled the pin on the grenade and threw it.

It bounced twice before disappearing under the front of the lead SUV. The vehicle hadn't cleared it when the explosion erupted, throwing the rear of the SUV into the air.

It crashed down and lurched to the left, ramming into a vehicle parked on the side of the street. It pushed the vehicle into the building behind it and came to a sudden stop.

Hawk brought up his 416 and opened fire on full auto at the second SUV. It came to a stop and shooters tumbled out as the doors were flung open.

They took up positions around the parked cars. Before too long there were eight on the street, all firing in the direction of the two Talon operatives.

Hawk dived behind a parked BMW on the left side of the street. He dropped his empty magazine, rammed home a fresh one, and then commenced firing. On the other side, behind a parked Audi, Gray did the same.

Bullets punched into the vehicle providing cover for Hawk. Further along the street he could see the shooters starting to leapfrog each other. It was obvious that they were military trained.

Hawk leaned around the rear fender of the BMW and squeezed off another short burst. One of the leapfrogging shooters went down in a tangle of arms and legs, a cry of pain escaping his lips. The man squirmed for a moment before one of his comrades broke cover to drag him by his collar back to safety. However, before the rescuer could make it, Gray fired and shot him dead.

Then out of nowhere a man appeared with an RPG on his shoulder. Hawk took a disbelieving look and shook his head. "You have got to be fucking kidding me. Marcus, RPG coming in."

With a *whoosh*, the rocket propelled grenade launched from its firing system, streaking along the street with a white contrail tracking its movement. Hawk threw himself backwards as the explosive struck the BMW and detonated on impact. The roar was loud, made even more so contained by the row of buildings lining the street. Windows up and down the street blew out from the force of the explosion. The former SAS operator felt a wave of heat wash over him from the blast.

Stunned by the concussive blast, Hawk lay back trying to gather himself. He let out a moan and rolled onto his side, head full of cobwebs. With a shake of his head to clear the fog, somewhere amongst the ringing in his ears he heard, "Jake, are you OK?"

"I've been better." Hawk groaned as he tried to get to his knees.

"Well, you better get your shit together because they're coming at us from both sides."

Swiping at his forehead, Hawk's hand came away slick with blood. He'd obviously received a cut of some sort above his right eye. He crawled around behind a parked vehicle to his rear, this time a Mercedes. He leaned against the door and gathered his breath.

"Jake, are you still with me, mate?" Gray asked as he opened fire once more.

"I'm here."

"I could use some help."

"Sorry, Marcus, that blast rang my bell a bit. I'll be right with you."

With a groan he came to his knees and brought his 416 up. Marcus had been right; he could see the shooters coming down both sides of the street, leapfrogging the parked cars.

Hawk shook his head once more in an effort to clear it

then started firing. The rounds exploded from the 416 and he saw the shooters on the left take cover behind what looked to be an Audi.

The front window shattered, and sparks flew off the body of the automobile. Hawk stopped shooting and took cover again. "Marcus, is that prick with the RPG still out there?"

"Did you shoot him?"

"No."

"Then he's still—"

BOOM!

A car on the other side of the street went up like a giant had kicked the hell out of it. It reared in a ball of flame before crashing back to earth.

"I've had enough of this shit," Hawk growled, peering around the Mercedes to see if he could find the attacker with the RPG. "There you are."

The suppressed 416 recoiled into Hawk's shoulder and the RPG man died, his chest torn apart by 5.56 rounds.

"That prick piss you off, Jake?" Marcus asked cheekily.

"Son of a bitch was trying too hard to kill me. Had to put a stop to it."

Suddenly another SUV pulled up and more masked shooters tumbled from it, opening fire immediately.

"Where the hell are these pricks coming from, Alpha One?" Hawk asked as he returned fire, his tone revealing his annoyance. "They're coming—"

Hawk grunted and went down.

"Bravo One, are you alright?" Anja asked.

Hawk groaned.

"Bravo One, can you hear me, over?"

Another moan.

"Bravo One, copy?"

A weak voice came over the net. "I'm hit. Man down."

GRAY HAD JUST SENT another shooter to St. Peter when he heard Hawk's voice. He turned his head and looked in his partner's direction as bullets punched into the vehicle he sheltered behind. "Shit. Jake's down, Alpha One."

"Do you have your Synoprathetic suits on, Marcus?" Anja asked.

"Yes, Boss."

The Synoprathetic suits were worn like a onesie under their normal clothes. It was an innovation of the Global Corporation's science department. The fabric was completely bullet proof but was unable to cushion the blow, putting the receiver down and out of commission for a time. It wasn't perfect but it saved lives.

Gray fired a burst from his 416 and ran across the street to check on Hawk. He found him conscious and in pain. "You all right, Mucker?"

"That shit bloody hurts," Hawk moaned with a cough to get his breath back.

"Time to get back in the fight, mate," the former para said as he fired another burst at the steadily advancing shooters. "No time for lying about."

"I'm in the wrong job," Hawk said, climbing to his knees. "I might put in for a transfer."

"Where to?"

"The frigging bar."

"RPG!" Gray shouted as another explosive lance came in.

The explosion threw them aside like rag dolls, slamming them onto the street and knocking the stuffing out of them. Both moaned and coughed to regain their breath. Hawk rolled onto his back and looked up to see a face behind a gun looking down at him in the orange streetlight. Hawk coughed and said, "Fucking do it, I hurt too much to care."

For a moment Hawk thought of Ilse, the one thing good in his life in a long time. Things were only just getting started and now he was about to die on his back in Naples.

CRACK!

The man's head snapped back in a spray of blood, his legs giving out like a marionette with its strings cut. Then came the sound of steady gunfire.

Hawk rolled to the side and looked. What he saw made him smile. "That's it, lass, give the bastards what for."

Slania was firing a CZ Bren2 with methodical ease and giving the shooters something to think about. Hawk struggled to his knees and saw the bodies already lying in the street. "Damn it, lass, you're a bloody sight."

"Just get your friend into the van and let's get out of here, Duck," she shot back at him.

He grunted. "Duck?"

"That's right, lame duck."

"Shit a brick. You're a keeper."

———

ILSE GAVE him a light kiss and said, "There, all better."

Hawk looked down at his torso then across at Gray. Each man had bruises, scrapes, and more than one piece of sticking plaster on them. "I don't feel better. How about you, Marcus?"

"I feel like you look, Mucker."

"You'll feel worse when Anja gets hold of you," Ilse said.

"It wasn't my fault," Hawk said defensively. "He was shot by his own people."

"Get dressed. Debrief in ten."

She left them to get their clothes on. Hawk looked at Marcus and said, "You want to do the debrief on your own?"

"Not bloody likely, mate."

"Yeah, how did I know you would say that?"

Once they were dressed the pair went out into the area set up for operations. The team were operating out of a store which had closed during the Global Financial Crisis. It had been picked up by a firm which was a front for MI6 who often let Talon use their safehouses across the globe. At a price.

Anja was waiting for them. She was seated on the corner of a desk. She looked up from a piece of paper she was reading and stared straight at Hawk.

Christ.

"Mr. Hawk, by my calculation your hearing must be totally shot. Am I right?"

Hawk was puzzled by the question. "Boss?"

"Your hearing. Is it all right or do we need to invest in a hearing aid for you?"

Beside him Gray stifled a chuckle. Anja glared at him. "Do not laugh, Mr. Gray. You owe the task force a van."

He snapped to attention. "Boss."

"Now, Jacob, I am still waiting for the answer to my question."

"No, Boss."

"No boss, what?"

"My hearing is fine."

Anja came to her feet and walked off to the side before stopping and staring at the far wall. When she turned back, her blazing eyes stared daggers into her charge. "Then what part of not stealing expensive vehicles do you not *understand*?" The pitch of her voice was an octave higher than her normal tone. Her mood was very dark.

"In my defense—"

"Save it. I don't want you to try to justify it. You stole a

17

million-dollar vehicle, and it ended in flames. A fucking Maserati. If a bloody Range Rover had been parked beside it, I'm certain that you still would have taken the Maserati. Well, no more. From now on, each and every time you steal a vehicle valued above twenty-thousand Euros, every euro will come out of what you are paid."

"Yes, Boss."

"Now we address the other issue. The fact that when given a mission to extract a target, you somehow manage to get them killed."

"Not my fault, Boss. His people shot him, not me."

"Your mission was to get him out alive so he could be questioned about the bounty on your head. To keep him safe. Yet here we are again with another HVT killed under your protection."

Hawk was starting to feel like a scolded child and couldn't help but look at the floor.

But Anja wasn't finished. She shifted her gaze to Gray. "You cost me a van."

"With respect, ma'am, that wasn't my fault."

Anja nodded. "Granted. But you let Sir Fucksalot talk you into abandoning it, so that makes you complicit."

"Boss."

"I expect better from my people. Next time around I shall get it. Now, we're standing down for a week or so. In the meantime, Slania will look to see if she can find another source leading to who put the bounty on Jacob's head. Until then, we're flying to Santorini. Enjoy your time off. And I shouldn't have to say this, but stay out of trouble."

CHAPTER TWO

Rio De Janeiro, Brazil

IT WAS BRIGHT, gaudy, and in your face. Semi-naked women clad in amazing costumes, floats, and up to 2,000,000 revelers per day enjoying Rio Carnival. One of whom happened to be a young British woman named Lila Farhadi, sharing the experience with her best friend, Paula Dennis.

Paula was the daughter of a London dentist. Lila's father was Akmal Farhadi, a billionaire who'd made his fortune in furniture, expanding his company across the globe. Originally from Pakistan, Akmal had sought a better life for himself and his family. One which they all now had.

Lila had inherited the darker skin of her parents but the accent of a Londoner.

"Isn't this wonderful?" Lila said to Paula, having to lean close to her friend's ear to be heard over the noise.

"It's bloody amazing is what it is."

Hands suddenly grabbed Lila from behind and a young man kissed her on the neck. "I'm back."

She tensed at first, taken by surprise, then the tension

went out of her, and she spun around. "You bastard, Emilio. You scared me!"

"I'm sorry," the young man apologized. He smiled, showing large white teeth. "Are you all right?"

She kissed him fiercely. "I'm wonderful."

He cupped her buttock with his hand. "Good, let's go and join in the fun."

Lila looked around at Paula. "Come on, Paula. Come with us."

Paula shook her head. "I'm going back to the hotel. I don't feel well."

Lila stared at her and realized she was lying. Maybe she felt like a third wheel. "Are you sure?"

"Yes, go and have some fun. We'll come out again tomorrow night."

Lila nodded. "All right."

Lila watched as Paula disappeared into the crowd. She turned back to Emilio and took his hand. "Come on, then, let's party."

They moved into the crowd and joined in the revelry. Dancing, shouting, hugging people Lila had never met before.

One woman in costume was painted from head to foot in gold. She wore feathers of different colors and her scant clothing was covered in diamond-like sequins. Another woman was dressed like a belly dancer, her costume decorated in colored jewels, and a headdress of large purple feathers hung down her back.

Following all the glitz and glamour of the costumes came the floats. One was a giant blue turtle, on top of which was a large platform with gaudy girls dancing. It was all about the dancing. It was Samba.

"This is just wonderful, Emilio," Lila said to him.

He leaned in and said, "Come, I want you to meet a friend."

Lila's eyes widened. "Sure, I would love to meet a friend of yours."

This was Lila's fourth day in Rio. She had met Emilio on the first night and the two had hit it off from the start. She had yet to meet any of his friends, so this was a great opportunity.

After a few minutes of dragging Lila through the crowd, Emilio took her into an alley mouth. He looked around for his friend, frowning. "He was meant to be here."

He looked around some more before turning back to Lila. "Wait here. I'll be back."

Emilio kissed her and disappeared into the crowd.

Lila moved closer to the alley mouth so she could see more of the parade. The streetlight made her eyes sparkle with happiness. Her lips formed a broad smile as she watched intently. Home was miles away, but Lila didn't care. This was way better than London. Way—

A dark hood slid over her head as someone pinned her arms to her side. Then before she could scream, her mouth was taped around the outside of the hood. She struggled fiercely, kicking. Then she managed to get an arm loose and she reached back, clawing at the face behind. The assailant cursed out loud and his instinct was to let go.

Tearing at the hood, Lila managed to get it off. Another assailant grabbed for her, causing Lila to lash out more. Her fingers became claws as she went for the eyes. *Blind your attacker and he can't hurt you.*

Flesh came away under Lila's nails, bringing forth a howl of pain. But instead of reeling away, he lashed out with a bunched fist. It crashed against Lila's jaw, knocking her sprawling across the alley. A large rusted bolt was protruding from the wall on the other side and Lila's head crashed into it, the impact dropping her like a stone. As she lay on the asphalt, her body quivered uncontrollably until it ceased to move at all.

"What the fuck have you done?" one of the attackers blurted out.

"Nothing. I just gave her a tap to quiet her down."

The first man stepped forward and checked Lila's pulse. "You stupid prick, you've killed her."

Santorini, Greece, 1 Week Later

Ilse lay beside the crystal-clear pool in a pink bikini, sunglasses on to block out the sun's glare. Hawk placed an ice-cold bottle of beer on her defined stomach before removing it again, causing her muscles to tense and jerk. "You bastard, Jake," she growled as goosebumps rose all over her body.

Hawk chuckled and handed it back to her. "You'll turn into a lobster if you keep roasting out here."

Ilse sighed. "You're right. Pass me my shirt, will you?"

"Hey, don't get too excited. I didn't say cover up that fine form of yours. How about some more sunscreen?"

"You're an idiot."

In the pool, Gray was on his fiftieth lap. Or was it five-hundredth? The man was a swimming machine and loved water. Hawk said, "I swear the bugger is a damn fish."

"You should be doing that, Jake," Ilse said. "Good cardio exercise."

"I get all the exercise I need, thank you."

"I'll say you do," Slania said. "The hotel walls aren't that thick, you know."

Hawk grinned broadly, but Ilse turned a bright shade of crimson with embarrassment.

Slania was lounging in a chair a short distance from them, her blue bikini revealing the true extent of her tattoos. She, like Ilse, had an athletic build and her form was a sight to behold.

"What's the boss up to?" Hawk asked.

"I think she got a call about something," Slania replied.

"About yours truly?"

Ilse rolled her eyes. "Not everything is about you, Jake."

He grunted and took a pull of his beer.

"Does that man ever stop swimming?" Anja asked as she appeared from inside the stark white villa where they were staying. She wore a pair of light cotton shorts and a red bikini top which revealed her bullet wound scars. Even with her sunglasses hiding her eyes, she looked the most relaxed she'd been in weeks.

Actually, they all had scars of some description.

"He's part fish, Boss," Hawk said. "I think he's starting to grow scales."

Ilse said, "This is such a wonderful spot. I could stay here forever."

"Good. Because I just bought it for the taskforce to use." That got their attention. "In our down time I can't imagine a better place to be."

Hawk grinned. "You're an angel, Boss. I could give you a big kiss."

"Try it, Mr. Hawk, and I will shoot you where you stand."

"Must have cost a chunk of change."

"A little over two million. But it's not like we can't afford it."

Hawk nodded. "All right, but just say, right, that the bad guys pay us a visit. It—"

"Shut up, Jake," Ilse said. "Don't even go there."

"So, I shouldn't worry about that dicker up on the hill watching us with binoculars, then?" Hawk said nonchalantly.

"Oh, Christ," Ilse said with a shake of her head.

"I saw him, too," Slania said.

"You all talking about the dicker up on the hill?" Gray called out from the side of the pool where he'd pulled up to.

"Am I the only one who hasn't seen him?" Ilse asked.

Hawk came to his feet and walked towards the villa. "Where are you going, Jake?" Anja asked.

"See a man about a dog, Boss. Instead of him coming to see me in my house."

Anja nodded. "First sensible thing you've said all day."

Gray climbed out of the pool. "Wait for me, Jake. I'd like to talk to him, too."

As they passed through the villa, both men grabbed their Glocks, which were with the others on a coffee table in the living area. They walked out the front door and turned right until they were out of sight of the person watching them. Then they started up the hill.

"Note to self, Jake," Gray said as they tramped up the rocky ground. "Bring shoes."

"Not fucking wrong."

They kept climbing until Hawk figured they were above the height of the man who was eyeing the villa. Then they began traversing the slope to get across to his position.

"There he is," Hawk said to Gray. "Let's get him."

Using stealth practiced over years of military training, the pair were able to get within meters of the watcher without revealing themselves. They both stood up at the same time and said, "All right, cock. What are you up to?"

Stunned, the man whirled, took one look at them, and said, "Bollocks."

————

"I—IT'S not what you think," the man stuttered.

"Then what is it?" Anja asked.

"I was sent here to hire you."

"How did you know we were here?"

"My boss is very resourceful," the man replied.

Hawk stared at him. "What is your name?"

"Jerry Reed."

Hawk grinned. Ilse said, "Don't say it, Jake."

"Hmm?"

"Jake."

"Is your boss the Bandit?"

Ilse sighed. "Shit."

The man stared at him. "My boss is Akmal Farhadi."

"The billionaire?"

Jerry nodded. "Yes."

"What does he want with us?" Anja asked.

"He will tell you that when he sees you," Jerry replied.

"He's coming here?" Hawk asked.

"No, you will have to go to London."

Hawk shook his head. "Not going to happen."

"He will pay one million pounds for you to show up to the meeting."

Hawk looked at Anja who was deep in thought. "Boss?"

"We're both going to London, Jake. The others can stay here until we get back."

"All right, I can't wait."

Anja smiled. "I bet. Who'd want to stay here forever?"

"Don't worry, Jake," Ilse said. "We'll keep the beer cold, and the pool clean for you."

"Thanks," he said dryly.

CHAPTER THREE

London, England

IT WAS A TYPICAL LONDON DAY. Rainy and windy with deep gray clouds overhead. Hawk and Anja climbed out of the Black Cab and walked across the sidewalk to the concrete steps leading to two large, reinforced sliding glass doors.

Anja was dressed in a skirt and jacket, business like. Hawk was in jeans and a shirt covered by a knee-length, weatherproof jacket. They had arrived at Heathrow the day before, then spent the night at a large hotel in the West End. While Hawk organized to catch up with some old SAS friends, Anja went to the theater.

The following morning, they met at breakfast in an understated dining room decorated in muted tones, where they ordered light meals. Hawk barely ate any at all, his hangover playing hell with his head. But the little bit of food had him feeling a lot better.

They crossed a marble-tiled floor and walked up to a reception counter at which two women and a man were dressed in suits. One of the women, a Sri Lankan girl with dark features and even darker hair, smiled revealing straight white teeth. "Can I help you?"

"I have an appointment with Mr. Farhadi. My name is Anja Meyer."

She looked down at the touch screen set into the countertop. Her fingers danced over it momentarily before she made eye contact once more. "Yes, here it is. Please take the lift to the top floor where you'll be met by Mr. Farhadi's assistant."

"Thank you."

They walked over to the bank of elevators and Hawk pressed the call button. Within moments the doors opened, and they climbed aboard. Hawk chose the button for the fifteenth floor and the car started its journey upward. He said, "Why would a furniture guy have a building like this?"

"I don't know, Jake. Why don't you ask him?"

"I just might."

The elevator dinged and the doors slid open. A young blonde woman waiting for them smiled and said, "Please come with me."

They followed her along the hallway, her tight dress hugging her form in all the right places. Anja looked at Hawk who was looking everywhere other than the woman's butt. Maybe Ilse was having an effect on the former SAS operator.

The hallway opened out into a large room, open plan, full of cubicles. At the end of the room was a floor-to-ceiling glass partition with a door. The woman stopped. "Mr. Farhadi's office is over there."

"Thank you," Anja replied.

They made their way along a narrow thoroughfare until they reached the glass wall. The man inside saw them coming and waved them in.

Hawk opened the door and let Anja walk ahead before he followed. The man at the desk stood up and greeted them. "Welcome to Farhadi Enterprises. My name is Akmal."

They all shook hands, Anja first.

"I'm Anja Meyer. Pleased to meet you."

"Jacob Hawk."

"Please, have a seat," Farhadi said, pointing towards two chairs on the other side of his glass desk.

They sat down and Anja asked, "What is it we can do for you, Mr. Farhadi?"

"I want you to find those responsible for the death of my daughter."

The ensuing silence was heavy.

"I'm sorry for your loss, Mr. Farhadi," Anja said. "But we don't really investigate murders. We are a team that fight people trafficking."

Farhadi nodded. "I had some of my people initially investigate the death, and at the time of her murder she was seen struggling with two men. I have been led to believe that they were trying to kidnap her."

"Where did this happen, Mr. Farhadi?" Hawk asked.

"In Rio. She went there with her friend to see the Rio Carnival. And now..." He struggled for words. "And now Lila is dead."

Hawk and Anja both knew it was possible. Brazil had a high sex trafficking rate, especially for transsexuals who were often forced into it and shipped to Europe to work.

"I will pay you twenty-million pounds if you can find out what happened and bring whoever it was to justice."

"You make us sound like mercenaries," Hawk said, eyeing the man.

"That isn't my intent. I just want justice for Lila and perhaps prevent it happening to anyone else."

Anja asked, "Is her friend back in the UK?"

"Yes."

"We will talk to her and then decide if we should become involved."

"All I ask is that you consider my proposal."

"Where will we find her?" Anja asked.

"I will have my assistant provide it for you on the way out. Thank you."

True to his word, Farhadi's assistant handed them the address as they left his office. Then as they walked to the elevator, Anja took out her cell and dialed.

"Hello?"

"Slania, dig up everything you can on Akmal Farhadi."

"Yes, Boss."

The call disconnected and Hawk said, "Don't trust him, Boss?"

"Not in the slightest."

———

PAULA DENNIS LIVED in a small flat in Soho. It wasn't much for the money that was paid but it was close to her work and that's what counted.

Anja knocked on the door and waited for the girl to answer. "Paula Dennis?"

"Yes, miss."

"My name is Anja Meyer, and this is Jacob Hawk. Akmal Farhadi said we might get a word with you. Is that all right?"

Paula nodded and backed into the hallway, indicating with her arm for them to follow. "Please, come in."

They went inside and she pointed to a pretty floral sofa before saying, "Please, have a seat. Would you like a drink? Coffee or tea?"

Anja shook her head as she sat down. "No, thank you. We won't keep you long."

"Okay. How can I help?" Paula moved to a single chair, tucking her feet under her.

"Just tell us in your own words what happened the night Lila died."

Paula hesitated and then told them about that night. When she was finished, Hawk asked, "Who was Emilio?"

"He was a guy that we met in Rio. He and Lila hit it off right away."

Hawk nodded. "Where was he when everything happened?"

"He was looking for a friend."

"When you first met Emilio, did he show any interest in you as well?" Anja asked.

Paula shook her head. "No, just Lila."

"Was there anything out of the ordinary that either of you noticed? Anyone following you?"

"No, we didn't see anyone."

"Is there anything else you can think of?"

"Not really."

Anja and Hawk stood up. "Thank you, Paula," Anja said. "You've been very helpful."

"Really? I don't feel like I have."

"You have, believe me."

Once they were outside, Hawk said to Anja, "She was targeted. That girl in there was prettier than Lila and they left her alone."

"I agree," Anja said. "We need to talk to Emilio."

"So, we're taking it, then?" Hawk asked.

"Yes."

Hawk froze and his expression changed as he stared across the street. "You're fucking kidding me."

———

FOUR MEN CLIMBED from the dark green Land Rover Discovery, brandishing weapons. Their leader stared at Hawk from across the street and he immediately knew what it was all about. He said to Anja, "Get out of here. This is about me."

The newcomers immediately opened fire, sending bullets scything through the air. Hawk and Anja dived behind a parked Peugeot and heard more rounds punch through its thin exterior.

A passing vehicle was sprayed with gunfire, its driver slumping forward as it ran off the street into a parked car.

"Days like these you wish you had a weapon," Hawk said.

Anja opened her coat, pulled up her dress to show more than a little thigh, and took a Heckler and Koch P30 handgun from a holster strapped to her thigh.

Hawk raised his eyebrows. "That'll do."

She came up from behind the vehicle and opened fire at the closest shooter who was crossing the street. She hit him twice in the chest plate, stopping him instantly. Then as he staggered, she shifted her aim and shot him in the head.

Moving her aim again, she was about to fire when she was forced back into cover by a shooter unloading a magazine in her direction. Hawk grinned. "I think you pissed them off, Boss."

She stared at him. "Really? You think?"

His grin broadened.

Suddenly, Anja took off her coat, followed by her high heels. Then she held out her P30 for Hawk to take. His smile faded. "You're not going to do something stupid are you?"

"What would give you that impression?" Anja asked, tossing him a spare magazine for the handgun.

"You know what, Boss? You're mighty sexy when you're pissed."

She rolled her eyes. "Boundaries, Jake. Now just shut up and start shooting."

Hawk came up and began firing at the first target he

saw, trying to suppress his fire. Then he changed aim and fired at the next shooter, eventually alternating between all three. Meanwhile, Anja came out from behind the Peugeot and ran towards the fallen shooter. As she reached him, she went low and scooped up his weapon. It was a Heckler and Koch MP7.

Without stopping, she ran towards a vehicle on the other side of the street, her back slamming against the SAAB's front door.

Hawk had caught her movements out of the corner of his eye and was impressed. He knew she had what it took in the field, but witnessing it was something else.

The slide on the P30 locked back as Hawk fired the last bullet. He dropped out the magazine and replaced it with the fresh one.

Across the street, Anja put the MP7 to work with short bursts. Another of the shooters fell as a couple of slugs caught him in the chest and throat. Hawk grunted with appreciation and then zeroed in on the next shooter.

The killer had turned side on to fire at Anja, leaving himself exposed. Hawk shot him twice, killing him.

That left one more.

Who turned and ran.

"No you don't, mate," Hawk growled and left the cover of the Peugeot and started after him.

"Jake, leave it," Anja called after him.

"Bullshit I will. The bastard's not getting away."

The man ran into an alley and disappeared.

Hawk followed him, rounding the corner cautiously, treating it as a trap. He could see the man halfway down the narrow thoroughfare. Apart from the two of them, the alley was empty so Hawk brought the P30 up and fired twice.

The man staggered and fell forward, shot in the legs.

Hawk walked towards him. The man rolled over and

fought to bring his gun to bear. Hawk shot him again. This time in the head.

The former SAS operator knelt beside the dead man and checked his pockets for ID. Of course there was none.

He took out his cell and took a photo before sending it to Slania. Then he saw the tattoo extending below the man's sleeve. "Son of a bitch."

He turned and walked out of the alley just in time for the police to show.

———

FORMER GENERAL MARY THURSTON escorted Anja and Hawk out of the Metropolitan Police building and into a dark blue Range Rover. The doors closed and the driver pulled away from the curb.

"OK, let's tell me why I'm here calling in favors and what's happening," Thurston said curtly.

"That would be me," Hawk said. "I have a twenty-million bounty on my head."

Thurston turned. "Who did you piss off?"

"It's a long queue, General."

"And somehow this shit all went down in the middle of Soho."

"Not my place of choosing," Hawk replied with a shrug.

"All right, so tell me why you're in London. The last I heard you were in Santorini."

Anja said, "We were here to talk to Akmal Farhadi, the furniture magnate."

Thurston nodded. "Didn't his daughter get murdered a week or so ago? It was in the papers."

"That's right. He wants us to find out who was behind it. It looks like a failed kidnapping. I'm reasonably sure she was targeted."

"Unlike you to take on a job for hire," Thurston said.

"If it's a kidnapping ring then we'll do it. It does smell that way."

The Range Rover turned a corner into a side street when a black Audi appeared and stopped in front of them. Then a screech from behind confirmed the second vehicle.

Hawk sat facing forward. "Did someone order a spook sandwich?"

The doors on the vehicle in front opened and four men climbed out. Thurston's driver looked at her and said, "What do you want me to do, ma'am?"

"Stand down, Brick."

The shaven headed man with the beard nodded. "Yes, ma'am."

Thurston climbed from the Range Rover and closed the door. A man with dark hair and wearing a long coat stepped forward to meet her. "Mary Thurston?"

Thurston nodded. "You seem to have me at a disadvantage."

"Simon Venables. Intelligence."

"Six or Five?"

"I don't think that matters."

"What can I do for you, Simon?" Thurston asked.

"I would like to talk to your two passengers," he replied.

"Couldn't you have done that at the Met?"

"Better this way."

Thurston turned and motioned to Anja and Hawk who climbed from the Range Rover and walked forward. Hawk looked behind them and saw the four men at their rear. They stopped beside Thurston and waited.

"Simon Venables here wants to talk to you," she explained.

"Could have called," Hawk said. "I'm sure he could have found the number."

"What is it you want, Mr. Venables?" Anja asked.

"I need to know why you are visiting Akmal Farhadi."

"Business," Anja replied.

"What kind of business?"

"Why do you want to know?"

"That is top secret," Venables replied. "Now, the answer is?"

Anja said, "Jake."

"Polite, Boss?"

"Yes, Jake. As you would a telemarketer."

He stared at Venables. "Fuck off."

One of the men with Venables went to take a step forward but the MI6 man held out a hand to stop him. "That isn't very polite, Miss Meyer."

"As I'm sure you are aware, I've had people trying to kill me today, been locked up, and now stopped by you. I'm not in a polite mood. Now, as you've stated, why you want to know is your business and I'm telling you, our dealings with Farhadi are our business. If we're done here, I have a plane waiting to take us back to Santorini."

"I could take you in forcefully and interrogate you, you know," Venables said.

"And all I have to do, Venables, is call your boss and they'll be released straight away," Thurston said. "And you will spend the duration in Scotland. We are done here, Mr. Venables."

The three of them turned and walked back to the Range Rover and climbed in.

Hawk put his belt on and said, "He might have been MI6, but the others weren't. SAS black ops."

"They seem awful keen on wanting to know your dealings with Farhadi," Thurston pointed out.

Anja nodded. "I've got Slania digging into his background. Even if we don't work for him, I would still like to find out what happened to his daughter and if we have a kidnapping ring to shut down."

"Just be careful," Thurston said. "I don't think that this is over yet."

Santorini, Greece

"You wanted to see me?" Ilse asked Slania who'd been working at her computer.

"Our dead guy that Jake sent me is a Russian. Name of Oleg Dorokhov. Former Special Forces. I tracked him and he has ties to Nikita Bondarev, an oligarch with friends in the Kremlin. But get this. Bondarev used to have a friend named Leonid Federov."

"Oh, crap," Ilse hissed. "And the bounty appeared around the same time Federov died."

"That's it."

"Get me what you can on Bondarev."

"Already got it," Slania replied. "Bondarev is an oil magnate with his own private army. They protect his interests in Iran, Syria, and a few other places. He's been known to hire his private army out on occasion when someone requires. I'm reasonably sure it was him who posted the bounty, but he's got people of his own hunting Jake, too. The fact that they found him in London means they are very high tech."

"Was there a link to our Italian friend?"

"Yes. Marco used to be in oil exploration before he turned to the dark side."

Ilse looked worried. "If they know about London then they know about this place. We need to put more security in."

"At least Jake isn't here," Slania said. "That way they'll leave us alone."

Gray appeared. "I think we may have a problem."

"What?" Ilse asked.

36

The power went out and everything turned dark.

"Shit," Gray growled.

Ilse said, "You can say that again. Come on."

Using the light filtering in from outside the building, they hurried through the villa to the garage. Ilse opened the trunk of the BMW X5 and revealed the lockbox inside. She punched in the key code and opened the lid. This was their home kit. MP5SDs, body armor, Glock handguns, and NVGs. Along with magazines of ammunition.

They took what they needed, and when they were ready, slipped on their night vision. Ilse said, "Gray, west wing, Slania, east. I'll take the other. Once you've cleared your sector, circle the perimeter, and meet near the pool."

"Roger that."

"And don't get yourself killed on my watch."

———

GRAY MOVED SILENTLY through the dark, the green haze before his eyes making everything that much easier. So far, he'd seen nothing sinister, but he was approaching the large games room where the billiard table was. Along one wall were French doors which swept back to bring the outside in.

He slid along the wall and peered around the corner. The doors were open. Someone was inside. Then he caught the movement.

The MP5 came around and he stroked the trigger. It spat a short burst and the intruder jerked before falling behind the billiard table.

Suddenly, Marcus was under suppressed fire from another shooter he couldn't see. He ducked back, and bullets stitched a pattern across the other side of the wall. He winced. Anja was going to go berserk.

He leaned back around the corner, locating the

shooter over near the bar. Bringing the MP5 around, Gray squeezed off another burst of fire.

The shooter moved evasively, and the bottles on the shelves bore the brunt of the burst, shattering and spraying glass and alcohol everywhere. Gray ducked back as the intruder fired again. More bullets hammered into the wall. "Fuck."

This time when he fired, it was a lot more accurate. The intruder cried out and fell back into the bar with a crunch. Gray moved from his position behind the wall and swept the rest of the room. It was clear.

Then the entire window wall shattered as machinegun fire ripped through it.

———

THE KNIFE in Slania's right hand cut deep through the intruder's femoral artery before coming up and plunging into his throat. Blood sprayed across the living room, dark and warm. She let him drop, reached for her Glock, and shot the second intruder in the chest. His armor plate took the full force of the rounds, but even then it was enough to take him to his knees.

Slania swiftly stepped forward and placed the handgun against his head and pulled the trigger.

The killer's head snapped back, and he fell backward, blood starting to pool on the cold tiles.

Then another shooter appeared and he opened fire with an automatic weapon. Bullets sprayed the living room, holes appearing in walls and the sofa. Slania hit the floor and rolled, coming up and firing the Glock. She missed but it threw the intruder's aim off long enough for her to fire again. This time she hit him center mass. His arms flailed as he fell back, in pain but not wounded.

The former Belgian special forces operator came to

her feet, walked towards the downed shooter, and like the other, shot him in the head.

That was when she heard the machinegun fire.

———

IN THE DINING area of the villa, Ilse had shot one of the intruders but the second caught her by surprise. He crashed into her from the side, sending her sprawling across the tiled floor. She lost her grip on the MP5 as it clattered away from her. But instead of trying to retrieve it she rolled onto her back and drew the Glock. It crashed in her fist three times, the first bullet hitting the intruder in the chest, the second in his throat, the third in the face, just below his NVGs.

She scrambled to her feet just as he hit the floor like a tree falling in the forest. Ilse remained on her knees while she swept the dining room. A third shooter appeared. "Fucking bitch," he cursed out loud, his accent thick.

He fired at Ilse as she rolled away to her left. Bullets cracked off the tiles and ricocheted into the walls.

Ilse came to a stop and fired at the shooter, a round clipping his shoulder. He cried out in pain but stayed in the fight. Once more his weapon fired, and Ilse dived under the dining room table. Bullets chewed splinters out of the wooden top, and some punched through. She crawled forward until she was almost clear, and the figure came into view. Ilse opened fire at the shooter's legs, crippling him. As he fell in front of her, she fired at his head.

With eyes wide in pain and shock, he died facing her.

Then came the machine gun fire.

She came out from under the table and climbed to her feet, rushing forward to slide the glass door open. To her right she could see the flashes from the machine gun lighting up the shooter's position.

Slania joined her. "He's got Gray pinned down. We need to flank him."

"Lead the way."

Slania walked around the pool, her MP5 up and ready to fire. Ilse came behind her, sweeping left and right as well as behind them. The machine gun went quiet, and Ilse guessed they were feeding in a new ammo belt.

Suddenly Slania disappeared and Ilse heard the suppressed MP5 rattle. Then nothing.

The former Belgian special forces operator appeared and said, "X-ray down."

The crunch of boots on glass signaled Gray's exit from inside. They turned and Ilse asked, "Are you all right, Marcus?"

"I'm still in one piece," he replied. "But that sure was intense."

Ilse nodded and looked back at the villa as sirens sounded in the distance. "Anja is surely going to be pissed."

CHAPTER FOUR

Santorini, Greece

ANJA LOOKED around at the state of the villa. "How is it that you always manage to piss someone off, Jake?"

"In my defense, Boss, this was not my fault," Hawk said. "But it's enough to make you weep."

Ilse said, "The repair people are coming later today."

"It is a good thing we're not short of money," Anja said. "Damn that Russian bastard. We need to put a stop to this."

"Are we going after him?" Hawk asked.

"First, we have to find him. In the meantime, I want everything made ready to go to Rio. We have a mission to prep for."

The others went about their business, leaving Hawk and Ilse alone. She wrapped her arms around him and kissed his lips. "I'm glad you're back and in one piece."

"Old Bullet Magnet Barney?" he said jokingly.

"Not funny, Jake. We need to get this sorted. People are coming out of the woodwork to collect this bounty."

He sighed. "You're right. Come on, Helga my love, let's get organized."

"Helga was from Sweden, Jake."

"I know."

———

THEY HELD a briefing later that day after the repair man had been and given his quote. The group sat outside near the pool and drank beer while they discussed the op. Anja started with Ilse. "Logistics?"

"The plane is prepped and loaded with our equipment, including weapons. I've been in touch with Brazilian Intelligence, and they've agreed to let us operate, provided we keep it under the radar. They're going to provide us with a liaison to help where they can and to keep us in our own lane."

"Where are we at narrowing down our number one suspect?"

Slania said, "I reached out to Paula to find out where they had been with Emilio. If you open your folders, you'll see a picture of the guy we're after. Cloud based security storage is a wonderful thing."

The picture was of a young, dark-haired man in his twenties. Also in the picture were Lila Farhadi and her friend Paula. Anja nodded. "Good work."

Hawk frowned. "I've worked in Brazil with MI6 before. Why does he look familiar?"

"The second picture. Juan Mendes."

"Oh, bollocks."

"You know him, Jake?" Gray asked.

"Yeah. Son of a local drug boss. Hard-nosed asshole. Ran across him back in fifteen."

"He's even more hard-nosed now," Slania said. "He virtually runs the Rio underground. Prostitution, drugs, sex trafficking. Throw in a few other things."

Hawk frowned. "Would this be a family business thing?"

"I'm glad you asked, my British friend. The short answer is no. Go to exhibit three."

Another picture, this one of two Caucasian males.

Gray said, "Definitely not family, which begs the question, why would Emilio help these guys?"

"He wants something," Anja said.

Slania nodded. "Quid pro quo. Juan Mendes was killed in a car bomb the day before yesterday. His son is now the big dog in town."

"Bollocks," Hawk growled. "It takes someone with skill to take out the top cartel boss in Rio. We need to talk to Emilio."

Anja nodded. "Yes, we do. Ilse, see if you can set up a meeting with our Brazilian friend."

"Yes, Boss."

"Jake, any idea how you want to play this if we can't get a meet?"

"Observe, then once we know his routine, we pick him up."

Anja said, "Sounds like a plan. Slania, dig deeper and see if you can find out who our mysterious friends are. All right, we leave in the morning. Enjoy your last night in paradise."

———

Rio De Janeiro, Brazil

Brazilian Intelligence set the Talon team up in an old, abandoned office complex towards the center of the city. Their liaison was a woman named Fabrizia Pinto. She was in her thirties, with walnut-colored skin, dark collar-length hair, and deep brown eyes. She carried a Heckler and Koch USP chambered for the .40 S&W round.

"I need details of what this is about," Pinto said to Anja. "Just to keep my superiors happy."

Anja nodded. "Just over a week ago, a British national was murdered at the parade. We believe those responsible were a couple of Caucasian males. We have also considered that she was targeted specifically. Our job is to find out who they are."

Pinto shrugged. "Kidnappings happen all the time in Rio. Why is this one special?"

"Her father is a very rich man and wants to know what happened to his daughter. But you already know that, if you didn't then there is something wrong."

She nodded. "Do you know who these men are?"

Anja shook her head. "No, but we believe there is one person in Rio who does."

"Who?"

"Emilio Mendes."

"Motherfucker. No—no, no, no. You cannot go near him. He is poison."

"We just need to talk to him, Fabrizia. He set the girl up to be kidnapped but something obviously went wrong."

"How do you know this?"

"We have pictures of him with the girl."

"What is your proof?" Pinto demanded, her face a mask of defiance.

"How about this. Two girls go to Rio for a parade. One is pretty, the other not so much. They meet a guy. One that could have any number of pretty girls he wants. But he chooses the not so pretty girl. She was targeted."

"That doesn't prove anything." Pinto folded her arms and shook her head.

Anja said, "Then a few days after the fact, the young man's father dies in a car bomb, and he, the son, inherits the lot. Now do you see what I'm saying?"

"You are saying that he helped whoever it was and in payment they killed his father?"

"Exactly."

"All right, say I believe you. How do you want to proceed?"

"We have a meeting with Emilio tonight at his strip club."

Pinto shook her head. "You will never come out of there."

"I'm not the one going in."

———

"WHAT IS it with girls and big tits?" Hawk asked Gray as they watched the show on the main stage.

"Are you concentrating on the target, Jake, or the show?" Ilse asked in his ear.

"You tell me, Ilse. Do you wish yours were bigger?"

Gray almost choked on his drink and immediately put his hand up to prevent it from spraying all over Hawk. "Fuck, Jake." He wiped his mouth and shook his head.

"Are you saying they're small, Jake?" Ilse asked.

"No, just right."

"Nice save, now concentrate."

He said, "The target is in a booth at the back right corner located beside what I assume is a rear exit. There are four bodyguards with him and three ladies of pleasure."

Gray said, "I count another four X-rays around the room, and possibly more that we haven't picked up yet."

"Copy. Proceed when ready."

In a battered van outside the strip club, Ilse was running comms and cams. Pinto was in the vehicle with her, but sat in front behind the wheel. Both were armed with Bren2s, just in case.

Hawk took a long drink of his whiskey, downing it all. He placed the glass on the bar and said, "Let's go and have a chat with our friend."

Both Talon operatives went in unarmed. There was no point trying otherwise. They were frisked at the door, and besides, they were just there to talk anyway.

As they were about to leave the bar, a waitress approached them. "You want a dance?"

Hawk shook his head. "No, thanks, we're here to see someone."

She smiled. "Maybe you want dance, yes?"

The former SAS operator stared at her. "That's a fucking terrible accent, luv. Now, piss off."

"I don't think you understand," the waitress said.

Hawk felt the muzzle of a handgun press into his stomach. He looked down at it and then said to Gray, "Where do you think she hid that?"

"I don't want to know, Mucker."

Hawk nodded. "What now, Princess?"

"We leave out the back."

Hawk grinned. "You're a little overdressed."

"Just move."

"Jake, what's going on?" Ilse asked over his comms.

"Alpha Two, I do believe that I'm being kidnapped."

"Fuck."

"Stand down, Alpha Two. We'll handle it."

The woman signaled for their earwigs. They handed them over and she dropped them in a drink.

"Now, shut up and move, Mr. Hawk," the woman sneered.

———

A NARROW ALLEY at the rear of the strip club contained garbage, boxes, three men, and a van. Hawk looked at Gray. "There must have been a fucking fire sale on vans in this town."

"Seems that way."

The woman slipped into a long coat while one of the other men covered Hawk and Gray with his own weapon.

"You want to tell me what's going on?" Hawk asked the woman.

"I'm saving an operation and earning some money on the side," the woman said, her British accent now evident.

"Twenty million is a lot of money, huh?"

"Yes, it is."

"Who are you people anyway?"

"No one special."

"Are you Six?"

"Connie, we're ready to go," one of the men said to the woman.

"You're making a mistake, you know."

"I'll worry about that later."

"I'd worry about that now." He looked at Gray. "Don't you think?"

"Yeah, I would."

"Just get in the fucking van," Connie growled, indicating with her gun.

"Anytime now, Ilse," Hawk said out loud.

Suppressed gunfire sounded and the first of the men dropped where they stood. Connie whirled to see what was happening but by then the third member of her team was also dead on the ground.

She froze, her hands slowly rising above her head. Turning back to face Hawk, she muttered, "Wow, I guess you got me."

Ilse and Pinto closed in behind her. Hawk held out his hand. "Give me a gun."

"Why?"

"I'm going to put a bullet in this bitch's head."

"No, let her go."

"What?"

"Let her go. There's been enough death tonight. Just go back inside and talk to the target."

47

"Forget it," Slania said over their comms. "The target has gone."

"Bollocks," Hawk growled.

Ilse stepped forward and got into Connie's face. She took a picture and said, "Get out of here before I change my mind."

Connie disappeared into the shadows, leaving her team on the ground where they died. Hawk looked at Ilse. "There was something a bit hinky with that."

"What do you mean?"

"She said she was after the bounty, but if that's true I'd already be dead. They wanted me dead but not publicly."

"She said, 'saving an operation and earning some money on the side'," Gray pointed out. "The bounty was secondary to the operation."

"Do you think she was MI6?" Ilse asked.

"Almost certain." Hawk suddenly had an idea. "Bloody Venables."

"Who?" Ilse asked.

"Venables, the guy we had an issue with back in London."

"The black ops man from MI6?"

"That's the bastard." Hawk looked at Ilse and nodded.

"Fine, but let's get out of here before any more of them turn up."

———————

HAWK AND ILSE lay together on two mattresses placed side by side. She ran a finger through the hair on his chest, stopping at a bullet scar before continuing. "What are you thinking about?" she asked.

"Work, I guess," he replied, idly running his hand through her hair. "It's hard to switch off sometimes."

Hawk stared at the ceiling. It was covered in graffiti, like three of the four walls. The fourth had a hole in it.

Their weapons were beside their beds as though they were in a combat zone.

Ilse said, "I'll reach out again tomorrow and attempt to get another meet with Emilio. I have my doubts whether it will happen. You may need to set up a tail."

Hawk nodded. There was always a danger with tailing someone. He thought back to one he'd worked with an MI6 officer when he was seconded from the SAS. They were in Mali following a known arms dealer, trying to nail down any consistencies in his movements so they could pick him up.

Two days into the tail they'd been made. Not that they knew it at the time. The first inkling they had was driving into an ambush of shooters with AK-47s.

The MI6 officer was killed while Hawk had managed to escape, with the arms dealer's men after him. He lost himself in the slums of Bamako. What had ensued was a game of cat and mouse for the next six hours as Hawk pitted himself against his hunters.

When it was over, eight of the arms dealer's henchmen were dead, and a Black Hawk had shown up with an extraction team on it and got Hawk out of the city.

"I'll need a vehicle. Something that's not a van."

Ilse laughed and bit his shoulder. "That's up to Anja. She handles the money."

"Speaking of the boss, has she mentioned anything to you about us?"

"No, why?"

"I thought she might have."

"Put it this way, Jake, if she thought it was interfering with our work, or she had a problem, she would not sit idly by."

Hawk said, "You're right. She's one to speak her mind."

"How do you feel about it?"

"You're starting to come across as insecure, Ilse," Hawk said.

"I just want to be sure you're not having second thoughts."

"Not me," he replied. He leaned over and kissed her. "I'm in this for the long haul."

CHAPTER FIVE

Rio De Janeiro, Brazil

HAWK SAT over a plate of bacon and eggs, with a coffee mug close to his right hand. He felt as though he'd slept on rocky ground and wished there was a masseuse he could visit to straighten him out. Maybe all his years of operating were starting to catch up with him. "Getting bloody soft."

Gray came and sat beside him. "Who would have thought there would be a breakfast house so close to the crib?"

"It's actually not bad food, either."

"What's the plan for today?" Gray asked.

"Ilse is going to try and set up a meet. If she can't, it'll be our task to work out a tail."

"Are you alright? You look like shit," Gray said around a mouthful of scrambled egg.

"Slept the wrong way."

"That'll do it."

They continued eating and were almost finished their coffee when three black SUVs pulled up outside the breakfast house, disgorging a handful of men.

"Heads up," Gray said, putting his coffee cup on the

table, reaching for his weapon. "Things could be about to kick off."

Hawk pushed his plate away with one hand and his coffee cup down with the other. He watched on with interest as three of the men entered the building. They turned and made their way straight towards where the two men sat.

"Fuck me."

"You know these people?" Gray asked with interest.

The man in charge slid into the seat next to Gray, forcing him to slide over. "Hello, Mr. Hawk."

"Fucking Venables. What do you want?"

"Just to have a friendly chat."

"What about?"

"A mutual friend of ours. Emilio Mendes."

"Did you send that bitch and her people after me last night?" Hawk asked.

Venables shook his head. "No, she did that all on her own. I was still in the air then. She's been sent for disciplinary action."

Venables' choice of words made Hawk wonder if he'd had her killed. "What about Mendes?"

"Stay away from him. You don't know what you're messing with."

"You came all this way just to warn us off? Is that it?"

"Something like that."

"Oh, piss off. I don't believe that for a second. What is he to you, Venables? Did you people take out his father?"

The MI6 man's eyes narrowed. "Leave it, Hawk."

"Are your people mixed up in the death of Lila Farhadi?"

Venables stood up. "Back off, Hawk. You're pissing in someone else's pool."

Venables turned abruptly and led his men from the establishment, brushing aside an elderly couple coming through the door. Gray nodded and said, "Nice cunt."

"But not useful."

Hawk's cell buzzed and he looked at the screen. "We have to go. They've got something."

THE OTHERS WERE WAITING for them when they returned. Anja stared at them as they entered and said, "Nice of you to join us."

"Where's the fire?" Hawk asked.

"While you two have been off tasting the local cuisine, Slania has discovered a few things of interest."

Slania stood up and walked over to a large screen. She pressed a button on her clicker and a picture of the woman known as Connie appeared. "Connie Granger. I believe you know her from last night."

Hawk said, "Yes. She's the MI6 cow."

"That's right. She was pulled out of the bay this morning with a bullet in the back of her head."

"Bloody Venables," he growled.

Anja stared at him. "Jacob, care to share?"

"Venables is in Rio. He put in an appearance this morning to warn us off Emilio Mendes."

"Interesting. Carry on, Slania."

"I did a dive on her before this news came through. She began her career as a soldier. Did time in Afghanistan before she was picked up by the Security Service. After a few years she was cut loose because she ordered the torture of a prisoner."

"Yet she's here, or was here, working for Venables and Six," Hawk pointed out.

"Yes and no. I think she was deep black. Her and her team. But that's where it gets interesting. Only one of her men was SAS, or former SAS. The others were from different countries. One was a Belgian, the other French."

"Sounds like a mercenary crew."

"It does indeed," Slania agreed. "More digging has them tied to Brian Warner."

Gray snorted. "This just gets better and better."

"I take it that you've had experience with Warner," Ilse said.

"Yes, ma'am. Sierra Leone. My company was operating as peacekeepers until the footsloggers could come in. We were QRF. About the same time, with the shit hitting the fan, the British Government decided to have Warner and his mercenaries take over security on the diamond mines. A group of rebels tried to hit one of the mines and got their bollocks handed to them. Warner's men captured ten prisoners. The following day they lined them up against a wall and executed them. The whole incident was swept under the rug and Warner was still handed contracts as they came around."

"They still could be," Hawk said. "We need to talk to Emilio. I bet my left knacker that those who tried to take Lila Farhadi were working for him."

"Do you think that's what Connie was doing?" Ilse asked.

"I don't know. We don't seem to be gaining any answers. Rather the contrary. The questions are compounding."

"You're right about one thing, though," Slania said. "Warner is involved somehow."

"Yes, but how?"

Anja said, "I suggest we find out. I want to know Warner's whereabouts along with those of any known associates that happen to pop up. Get onto it."

———

TWO MEN WALKED TOGETHER under the forest canopy on the outskirts of the city. Their position was encircled by a perimeter of strategically positioned shooters to prevent anything unforeseen from happening.

"This is getting messy, Brian," Venables said to the man beside him. "It's getting noticed."

Warner was former special forces who made his fortune on the black market after discharge. Quickly amassing enough money from illegal arms sales, he was able to set up his own mercenary company. From there he reached out to an old friend who helped him gain government contracts for his own country. Even when things turned ugly, Venables had been there to help clean up the mess.

"How was I to know the stupid cow was going to get greedy? Anyway, it's been taken care of, as you know."

"But we still have the problem of Talon. When we started this new venture, you assured me that things would be different. Yet here I am, halfway across the fucking world sorting your shit out once again."

"As you know, Simon, things don't always go to plan. The Farhadi thing was just an anomaly."

"An anomaly that could bring everything undone. I want you to get your people together and leave Brazil. I have another target for you. She is in Morocco. I'll have everything you need forwarded to you."

"What about Talon?"

"I'll have my people keep an eye on them. Just don't bugger up this next job or it might be the last."

———

THE HOME of Emilio Mendes was on the outskirts of Rio amid a tropical setting, surrounded by jungle. There was a long lap pool out the back on a landing which overlooked part of the city itself.

As the vehicle Hawk and Ilse were in passed through the large automatic double gates, the former SAS operative made mental notes of cameras and guards just in case he needed the intel at a future point.

"Someone is rich," Ilse said.

"He is now," Hawk agreed.

They pulled up at a turn around at the top of the driveway opposite some stairs down which two armed men walked to greet them. They were both frisked and then escorted inside.

The mansion was modern, with clean lines, and a basically open plan. The two armed guards escorted them through a minimalist living room and out to the landing which boasted a large pool. There, waiting on a sun lounger amidst a bevy of beauties, was Emilio Mendes.

"Told you," Hawk said out of the side of his mouth.

"Shut up."

"Welcome," said Emilio expansively, indicating with a sweep of his arm that they should remain standing because they wouldn't be there long. "I guess you know who I am, but I do not know who you are."

"Just call us Bill and Ben."

Emilio raised his eyebrows. "Flowerpot men?"

"Tank engines."

"I see." He eyed them suspiciously. "So, Bill and Ben, what can I do for you?"

"We're just here to ask a few questions and then we'll be gone."

"Okay?"

"Did you set Lila Farhadi up to be kidnapped?" Ilse asked.

Emilio smiled guiltily. "Why would I do that?"

"We're not here to judge you, Emilio. We just want to know what happened to Lila."

"I can neither confirm nor deny my involvement in such matters," he replied, smiling.

Hawk's face remained passive. *Smug prick, let's see how you deal with this.* "We have pictures of you with the girl in question just before she was killed. Then a few days after the fact, a car bomb kills your father. Now, you don't have to look too far to join the dots. You did something for them, they did something for you. Straight forward if you ask me."

Emilio glared at Hawk. "Nobody asked you, so be careful, my friend. I don't think you quite fathom who it is you are talking to."

"I know who I'm talking to, Emilio. Does the name Connie mean anything to you?"

There was a flicker in his eyes. "No."

Lies.

"Did she come to you asking to set the girl up for them to take her off the street?"

"No."

He's becoming agitated.

"Did she offer you something you couldn't refuse, Emilio? Did she offer to kill your father if you helped them out?"

"No!" He came to his feet, nostrils flaring. "I have had enough of this—these insults. You will leave now before I have my men shoot you."

Ilse said, "Before you give that order, Emilio, look down at your chest."

Emilio dropped his gaze and saw the pinpoint of the red laser sight fixated just above and to the right of his left nipple. His head snapped up, an expression of anger on his face.

Ilse said, "You don't think we would come here unprepared, do you?"

"You would not dare," he hissed.

"Bravo Two."

The whistle of the 7.62 round's approach could be heard faintly before the crack and then the explosion of glass as the water-filled vessel disintegrated on the small table.

"As you can see, Emilio, we are serious. All we want is a couple of answers and then we will be gone, and you can go back to running your kingdom by yourself."

His mask of fury was evident to them both, but it soon became obvious that Emilio resigned himself to the fact that he had no choice. "Fine. The woman came to me and asked me to set the girl up."

"Why?" Hawk asked.

"She did not say." They found no evidence of a lie on his visage.

"And you agreed."

"Eventually. But understand me, I was told the girl was not to be harmed."

"Yeah, well, she was," Hawk said. "Just so you know, Connie was pulled out of the bay with a bullet in the back of her head. Know anything about that?"

"I guess her employer didn't like failure." He shrugged and shook his head.

"I guess not. Be seeing you, Emilio."

They were escorted back through the house to their vehicle. Once they were inside, Ilse said, "That just confirms our suspicions."

"Yes, it does. Our next task is to find Warner."

"Easier said than done," Ilse replied.

"WARNER WAS in Rio up until an hour ago," Slania said. "Then I lost track of him."

"Do you know what he was up to?" Anja asked.

"Not really. He was good at covering his tracks. But I do have a destination. Morocco."

Anja frowned. "What is in Morocco?"

"There is something else. Something rather troubling."

"I'm listening."

"I've been doing some crosschecking and I can place

Warner, or his people, in countries where a number of young women—high profile, young women—were kidnapped and are still missing."

"Can you do me a profile on each of them for the team?"

"Yes, ma'am."

"Thank you. Let me know when you're done."

"Yes, ma'am."

Anja left her to it and went back out to the briefing room where the others were debriefing. Hawk looked up at Anja. "When are we leaving, Boss?"

"Soon. There are a few more things I want to check on before we go. However, it won't hurt to be ready."

Eyes turned towards the doorway as Pinto entered the room. There was a look of concern etched on her face. "I have some troubling news."

They waited for her to continue.

"An hour ago, the Rio police got a call about trouble at Emilio's home. When they arrived, it was like a war zone. Everyone was dead, including Emilio."

"Any idea who it was?"

Pinto held up a thumb drive. "It is all on here. They were able to get this off the security feed."

Ilse took it and within moments had it on the big screen. At first it was just guards and Emilio by the pool with his ladies. Then one of the guards near the gate fell, followed by the second. Then the shooters appeared. Six of them, dressed in black, masks on, and armed with suppressed AK-12s.

"These blokes mean business," Gray said.

They watched on as the well drilled team took out all the guards before reaching the pool area. Once there they shot the girls. Ilse drew in a sharp breath.

"Fucking bastards," Hawk growled.

Then the armed men took up positions around Emilio.

There was a discussion and then the young cartel boss was shot by each of the gunmen.

"What the hell did we just see?" Hawk asked.

"It looks like someone else just entered the party," Anja said.

"Could they be shooters from someone trying to take over the cartel?" Hawk asked Pinto.

"Unlikely. They were too well drilled. Had it been another cartel, it would have been much messier to send a message. This was an execution."

"Great, now we've got three problems. Bounty hunters, MI6 and Warner, and these wankers."

"Technically that's four," Ilse said.

"Four too many. Request permission to go back to Santorini and lay by the pool?"

"Sorry, Jake," Anja said. "Morocco calls. I also need to update Mr. Farhadi on the new developments."

"Shit."

Gray said, "Cheer up, Jake. Morocco has some great beaches."

"The last time I was in Morocco some prick was trying to kill me."

"Another of your friends, Jacob?" Anja asked, her eyebrow raised in question.

"Karim Belarbi."

"The terrorist?"

"That's the one. I was involved in an op with Six. We had Belarbi nailed down in Rabat. Anyway, he turned the tables on us and set a trap for yours truly."

Gray grinned. "Did you get out of it?"

"No, I fucking died."

"So that was you?" Anja asked. "You killed Belarbi?"

"Eventually. He and his people captured me. They were going to torture me and cut my head off. It was the in thing to do around that time. But I managed to escape and take Belarbi out at the same time."

Anja nodded. "There was one other thing. Slania has found a connection with Warner and a few other kidnappings across the globe. I'll update you when we have more. Until then, let's prepare to leave."

———

Somewhere Over the Atlantic

Slania sat down next to Anja and said, "I have something."

They were six hours into their flight and down below, looking out the window, one could see the whitecaps on the dark ocean from the wind whipping them up. Hawk was asleep, Ilse beside him looking through some intel paperwork, and Gray was listening to music through his headphones while drinking a bottle of water.

"What is it?"

"Three names so far. Aamani Singh, Indian, twenty-two, came from London, abducted in France. Father was a rug manufacturing multimillionaire. He was found dead of a suspected heart attack. The girl never surfaced. Reem Saleh, Saudi. She was twenty-three when she went missing from Scotland of all places. She was up there visiting with her family from London. Her father had ties to Saudi Oil. Not long after she disappeared, he was found dead. Once again, a suspected heart attack. The third girl is Heba Hassan. Egyptian, twenty-two. She and her family lived in London. Her father was in real estate. She was taken from a holiday villa in Spain with friends. Not long after—"

"Her father died of a suspected heart attack," Anja finished.

"Yes. None of these girls have been located."

"I'm starting to see a pattern. Something links all these girls, but what?"

"I think we should throw Lila Farhadi in that same basket, too," Slania said.

"Agreed." Anja thought for a moment. "Find me the next target. I need to talk to Frank Fitzgerald. He must know something."

The call rang three times before the connection went through. "Fitzgerald."

"Anja Meyer, Frank."

"Miss Meyer, how are things?"

"A little troubling, actually. I was hoping you would be able to shed some light on a few things."

"I'll try."

Anja went on to tell him about the missing young women and their fathers having heart attacks. "I think someone is using the girls to take their fathers out. Everything at this time points to a deep black operation inside of MI6. What can you tell me?"

"What were the fathers' names?"

Anja looked at Slania who was buried deep in her computer. "Slania, I need the names of the girls' fathers."

"Anjor Singh, Omar Saleh, and Montu Hassan."

"Did you get that, Frank?"

"Yes, wait one."

A few moments later, Fitzgerald came back to them. "All right, all three names are on the watch list."

"They're terrorists?"

"Not exactly, but they are suspected of financing terror organizations."

"What about Akmal Farhadi?"

"On the list also. At the top, actually."

"*Scheiße!*"

"Problem?"

Anja told him about Lila Farhadi. "Do you know Simon Venables?"

"I've had little dealings with him but I've heard things. He is in charge of Six's off the books work. Travels around with an SAS entourage and hires private contractors to do the heavy lifting so it can be deniable."

"Like Brian Warner?"

"Exactly like Brian Warner."

"Dear god, I'm starting to get a bigger picture of this thing and I don't like it."

"Be careful, Miss Meyer. Venables is not a person to be taken lightly."

"Neither am I, Frank. Neither am I."

CHAPTER SIX

Rabat, Morocco

ANJA REACHED out to an old friend at the Moroccan embassy who'd spent ten years in German intelligence for a place to set up their crib. In the end they'd found themselves in a large villa sharing it with German intelligence and the French Directorate-General for External Security.

The villa itself was rather large. Twelve rooms, spacious grounds, a swimming pool and two operations rooms where their staff could operate.

"I think I like this place," Hawk said to Ilse as they walked past the pool. "Sun and beer."

"We're here to work, Jake," she said.

"One can but dream," he replied with a sigh.

Anja appeared. "I have news."

Hawk rolled his eyes. "Don't tell me, we've got to go to work."

"Not just yet. Soon. We have a name. Kaaya Ismat. She is a young doctor doing volunteer work here in Morocco. Her father is Jaalib Ismat. He is a Libyan refugee who arrived in London twenty-five years ago with his young family. He is also, like the others, on the terror watch list for sponsoring terror organizations. We need to find her before Warner's people do. Slania is looking at hospitals. I need you two to check any refugee camps outside Rabat."

"Isn't she registered?"

"Yes, but they won't give out her information."

"Did you tell them—" Hawk stopped. "It was a stupid question anyway. We'll go and look."

"What should we do if Warner's men show up?" Ilse asked.

"No shooting unless they shoot at you. I don't want this getting out of hand. If you find her, and they try to take her from you, protect the package at all costs. On second thoughts, take Marcus with you."

"We'll need wheels."

She tossed Hawk a set of keys.

"I hope it's not a bloody van," he responded, looking down at the keys.

"You'll be happy to know it's a Toyota Land Cruiser," Anja replied.

Hawk smiled. "Great. A real bloody set of wheels."

––––––––

"FRIGGING PIECE OF SHIT," Hawk growled.

Gray chuckled and slapped Hawk on the back. "Cheer up, Jake, at least it's not a van."

"Shut up before I shoot you in the face."

The Land Cruiser had dents and needed a good clean. It looked more like something that Hawk had already gone a few rounds in rather than something that Anja had just bought. "I swear that woman hates me."

Climbing in, they stashed their handguns under the seats. After turning the key, the beast roared to life, and they spent the next twenty minutes driving out of the city to a large refugee camp which resembled a tent city. When they pulled up at the outskirts of the camp, they climbed out, taking their weapons with them. Ilse said, "We'll split up and see what we can find. Do you have your pictures?"

"Yes."

"Good. Meet back here in an hour."

Ilse walked between tents, taking it all in. She'd seen some bad camps in her time but nothing like this. The place was a slum; it stank and was full of flies. Disease was rife and sickness everywhere.

Every now and then she would stop and ask if anyone knew Doctor Kaaya Ismat. It wasn't until she asked the sixth person that she got a positive answer. "Excuse me, do you know this person? She's a doctor?"

The woman had limited English. She pointed to a large covered area thirty or so meters away. "Over there, over there."

Ilse nodded. "Thank you."

The covered area was the best attempt at a makeshift hospital. Nurses fussed over the sick and battled flies while they were at it. Instead of healing the sick, it was spreading the diseases quicker than they could be stopped.

Ilse approached a nurse and said, "I'm looking for Doctor Kaaya Ismat. Is she here?"

"Not here, love," replied the woman in a British accent. "Have a look over at the mess."

"Where's that?"

She pointed in a southerly direction. "Try over that way."

Ilse thanked her and walked in the direction the nurse had pointed before she went back to her futile task.

Up ahead Ilse saw another large tent. Raising the entry flap, she ducked her head to walk through, and when she straightened, she saw rows of tables but only two people seated at them. Ilse picked out Kaaya and walked over to the table. "Doctor Kaaya Ismat?"

Kaaya looked up from her meal. "Yes?"

Ilse could see that she was tired, her smock stained with sweat from the heat. "My name is Ilse Geller. I'm from a task force called Talon. I need you to come with me right away."

The doctor looked confused. "What? No. I'm not going anywhere with you."

"Doctor, I know this might seem strange—"

"It's not strange, it's unheard of."

"I'm sorry but your life may be in danger and—"

"Alpha Two, I've got multiple X-rays searching the camp."

It was Hawk. "Copy, Bravo One. I have the package. Rally back at the Land Cruiser."

"Package? Rally? Bravo One? What is this bullshit?" Kaaya was now angry.

"Listen to me," Ilse said hurriedly. "Your life is in danger. There are people here looking for you. If they find you, they will take you. You must come with me."

"No. I will not come with you."

Two men entered the tent. One was large, and broad-shouldered. The second was average height and build with dark hair. Both had the look of ex-military. Immediately Ilse knew they were too late.

The newcomers walked over to where the two women were and the big guy said, "Doctor Ismat, you need to come with us right now."

"I don't think so."

"Sorry, you don't have a choice," the second man said and produced a suppressed handgun.

"Hold on," Ilse said as she reached behind her back.

"No," said the man with the handgun and shot her.

The bullet hammered into Ilse's chest and knocked her back. As she fell she crashed into a table. Stunned, she lay on the floor, her Synoprathetic suit having saved her life. Not that the shooter knew that. To him she was down and out of the fight.

"What have you done?" Kaaya gasped.

The bigger of the two men stepped forward, grabbed her by the arm, and dragged her forcefully to her feet. "Move, now."

They hustled Kaaya from the tent and neither saw Ilse roll over. "Fuck, that hurts."

"Ilse, what's going on?" Hawk asked through her comms.

"They've got the package, Jake. Two men, both armed. One of them shot me."

"Are you alright?" His voice was calm and professional.

"Yes, thanks to the suit."

"Where are you?"

"Almost in the center of the camp."

"I'll be there in a moment."

"No, save the doctor," Ilse gasped, dragging herself to her feet. "Alpha Three are you on comms?"

"Copy, Alpha Two."

"Two X-rays have the doctor. I need you to find them before they get away."

"I'll do what I can," Slania replied.

"That's all I ask." Drawing her Glock, Ilse took a lurching step forward. "Fuck!"

———

HAWK HURRIED through the camp towards where the Land Cruiser was parked. It was the only place the kidnappers could park so it was obvious that was where they were headed. The problem was, there were possibly six or so of them and that would have him outgunned. Not that it would make any difference.

As he walked between two tents, he caught sight of the kidnappers escorting the doctor two rows over. She was struggling but they were too strong and well versed in what they were doing.

"I've got eyes on," Hawk said.

"Bravo One, I've got four more X-rays moving to join with the main target. Suggest you move a little faster."

"Copy."

Hawk took his Glock from his waistband and let it hang by his thigh. He turned to his left and moved stealthily across to the row the kidnappers were taking the doctor.

Reaching that row, he paused to make sure they were still moving forward. Hawk emerged and set off after them, quickening his pace.

Neither kidnapper was aware of his presence until he was on top of them. Hawk raised his weapon and shot the man on the left in the head before doing the same with the one on the right.

BANG! BANG!

It was that simple.

Kaaya yelped at the sudden noise. Too late to be of any use, her hands flew to her ears then her mouth when she realized what had just happened. She stared down at the dead men in horror. Meanwhile, Hawk said, "Alpha Three, I've got two X-rays down. Where are the others?"

"You need to get out of there, Jake. They're coming in on your—"

BANG! BANG!

"Bollocks!" Hawk exclaimed and grabbed Kaaya by the hand. "Come on, move."

They ran between the tents, desperately trying to lose their pursuers. Gunfire erupted once more, causing the refugees in the immediate area to run for cover.

"Who are these people?" Kaaya shouted at her savior.

"Kidnappers, lass. They want you to get to your father."

"Why?"

"No time to explain now. Just keep running."

Suddenly Kaaya tripped and fell. Behind Hawk gunfire sounded again. He whirled and brought the Glock to bear. He snapped off three fast shots in their pursuers' direction, causing them to scatter.

Kaaya came to her feet and shouted, "Stop shooting, you'll hit a refugee."

"Keep running lass, move."

"Jake, where are you?" Gray asked.

"I'm about thirty meters short of out ride, Marcus."

"Right, I'll meet you there."

"Ilse, where are you, girl?" Hawk said.

"Paralleling your track, Jake. I'll be with you—"

BANG! BANG! BANG!

"I'll be with you shortly."

"Are you alright?"

"No, I bloody hurt. These Synoprathetic suits might stop bullets, but they sure as shit don't stop the pain."

Hawk grinned to himself. "Welcome to the club."

As they reached the perimeter of the refugee camp, Gray appeared. Hawk said, "They're on our six."

One appeared and he started shooting. The man ducked back but was soon joined by the others.

The two Talon operatives along with the doctor reached the lot where all the vehicles were parked. As they did, Hawk noted that only three shooters came forward into the open. Then he noticed something else.

Ilse.

She came out behind them and opened fire. She shot the first shooter, then proceeded to take out the next two. All three fell to the dusty ground, squirmed, and then died.

Ilse jogged forward. Kaaya stared at her in disbelief. "You're alive."

"I'll tell you about it when we get moving," Ilse said.

They climbed into the Land Cruiser, Hawk behind the wheel. Starting the vehicle, he put it into gear. When he looked up, he saw a cloud of dust coming towards them. At its base were two technicals with mounted machine guns. His hand slammed against the wheel. "You have got to be shitting me."

Ilse leaned to the center of the rear seat and stared out through the window. "Alpha One, we've got a problem."

"Roger, Alpha Two. We're working on it."

"If you could, Boss, work faster."

Then the machine guns opened fire.

————

"GET ME A BIGGER GUN," Gray snapped as he saw tracer rounds coming in. "Jake, this situation calls for some of that crazy-assed shit driving you're known for."

"Crazy-assed I can do," he said as he yanked on the wheel and the Land Cruiser left the road.

Ilse leaned over into the rear compartment and grabbed a Bren2 along with some spare magazines. "Here, Marcus."

Gray took the weapon and rolled down the window. All within the vehicle felt the impact of rounds into the SUV as it bounced over the uneven ground. "Jake, I can't see them, turn."

Hawk turned so Gray could bring the Bren2 to bear and the former para opened fire.

The lead chase vehicle swerved, throwing his machine gunner's aim off. Not that it mattered because the rounds still found the Land Cruiser, shattering windows.

Ilse pushed Kaaya down. "Keep low."

"Who are these people?"

"I'm not sure." Ilse checked in with the crib. "Alpha One, any idea who these X-rays are?"

"We've been able to intercept some chatter, Alpha Two. They're not Warner's mercenaries. They sound German."

"More shooters after the bounty?"

"That would be my guess."

"Fuck, I hate hi-tech," Ilse growled.

"My thoughts exactly. Hold tight, there is help on the way."

"How far out?" Ilse asked.

"Air asset is ten mikes out."

"Copy. Jake, we've got an air asset ten mikes out."

"Wonderful. Now all we have to do is stay alive that long."

"Don't shoot the messenger, Jake," Ilse growled, turning in her seat then climbing into the rear compartment.

Next thing she had another Bren2 and was firing it, blowing out the rear window. "What the hell are you doing, woman?" Hawk shouted.

"They pissed me off."

"Don't take it out on the boss's wonderful machine." The sarcasm was thick.

"Shut up and drive."

More rounds from the technical hammered into the Land Cruiser, creating the sound of a hailstorm. Ilse canned fire discipline and emptied a full magazine at the lead vehicle, shattering the windshield into fine particles. The passenger jerked as bullets punched into him, and Ilse grunted with satisfaction. "Asshole."

Things went from bad to worse as one of the tires on the Land Cruiser was hit. Hawk fought to control the machine, but it was no use. The rim dug in and turned the wheel violently to the left. That was when the Land Cruiser rolled onto its side.

"That screwed that," Hawk said as the Land Cruiser started to settle. "Is everyone all right?"

Ilse had recovered first and scrambled free through the rear window. She took cover behind the wreck and opened fire once more. "Everybody get out!"

Gray helped Kaaya out through the back while Hawk climbed out through the top. He ducked around behind the Land Cruiser and drew his Glock. He looked at it and sneered. "Frigging pop gun."

Ilse retained her rate of fire, targeting the tires of the lead vehicle. Both blew and it lurched to a stop, causing the next technical in line to slide to a halt behind it. Men jumped clear and took up firing positions.

"I count six shooters, Jake," Ilse called out.

"Alpha Two, you have two more vehicles full of X-rays coming up behind the others," Slania said.

"I could do with some good news about now, Alpha Three," Ilse replied.

"The air asset is seven mikes out."

"Shit."

Gray put Kaaya in a safe place behind the Land Cruiser and joined the fight. Meanwhile, Hawk was looking around their rear for a safe exfil. "Alpha Three, how far out are those X-rays?"

"Two mikes, maybe less."

Two minutes.

"Alpha Two, am I seeing a drainage ditch to our rear, over?"

"Roger that. It looks like it runs a considerable distance and offers cover."

"Copy. Ilse, we're going to fall back to the drainage ditch at our rear. You go first and take the doctor with you."

"Copy."

"Marcus, cover me. I need to get the weapons bag out of the back."

73

"Roger."

Hawk edged along the vehicle to the rear. The smell of leaking diesel was strong near the fuel tank. He tapped Ilse on the shoulder. "You ready?"

"Yes."

"Doc, go with Ilse. Keep your head down and run like hell into that ditch."

"I really wish I'd never seen you people," she shouted over the gunfire.

"I wish that, too," he agreed. "Ilse, go, go, go."

With Kaaya in tow, both keeping their heads down, Ilse guided her into the drainage ditch twenty meters to their rear. While she did this, Hawk retrieved the weapons bag. Once he had it, he removed the third Bren2 and loaded a round into the chamber. "Take the bag, Marcus, and go. I'll cover you."

The former para picked up the bag and called out, "Moving."

Hawk commenced a round of suppressing fire, trying to keep down the heads of the attackers. "Jake, I'm in cover. Your turn."

Hawk looked back and saw that Gray was indeed in the drainage ditch and was waving to him to come over. The former SAS operator fired one last burst and said, "Stuff it."

Then he ran like the hounds of hell were chasing him.

———

HAWK SLID into the drainage ditch with a splash. A string of bullets chasing him chewed into the lip of the bank. He looked at the others. Both Ilse and Gray were firing at the attackers.

Hawk dug into the bag and found what he was looking for. Fragmentation grenades.

"Marcus," he called out and tossed him a couple. Then he repeated the process with Ilse.

Two additional SUVs arrived and disgorged their passengers. The three Talon people concentrated their fire on the new arrivals, making them think twice about pushing too far forward. Looking past the Land Cruiser, Hawk had an idea.

He took a grenade, pulled the pin, and threw it at their wounded vehicle. "Frag out!"

It exploded with a roar and was engulfed with flames as the diesel caught. Unlike a petrol engine, it didn't explode, but burned black creating a perfect smokescreen.

"Now what, genius?" Gray asked. "We can't bloody see them."

"Get your grenades ready, they'll be through in a minute. Alpha, how long before the air asset shows?"

"Three mikes, Bravo One."

"Copy."

"Here they come, Jake."

"Ready?" Hawk pulled the pin on his grenade. The others followed suit. "Frag out!"

All three threw their grenades, which exploded soon after they landed. The four attackers out front were blown off their feet from the multiple blasts.

"That'll work," Hawk grunted as he started firing at a new threat.

"I'm low on ammo, Jake," Gray said.

"Me, too," Ilse joined.

"Alpha, how far out—"

Suddenly the air was torn apart by the sound of a Giat 30 Revolver Cannon attached to the chin of a Eurocopter Tiger and the cries of the dying. Hawk rolled over onto his back and said into his comms. "Never mind, Alpha, it's here."

CHAPTER SEVEN

Rabat, Morocco

"THE SECOND GROUP of attackers were as we suspected. Bounty hunters," Anja said. "They seem to be popping up everywhere. Somehow, they're tracking our movements."

"Did the doc get away?" Hawk asked.

"The French are taking her to the airport as we speak. They've been really helpful."

"So, now what, Boss?"

Anja sighed. "I know you want to go after Bondarev but first we need to finish what we started."

"In the meantime, we have to deal with pricks appearing from behind the bushes."

"I'm afraid so."

Hawk took a sip of his beer and pulled a face. "This tastes like shit."

Anja smiled. "You'll be happy to know that since our little event yesterday, I managed to secure another vehicle."

"The way we're going through them lately, Boss, it better be a tractor."

"Not quite, dear. This time I managed to find a Humvee."

He nodded, impressed. "I like it."

"I've been meaning to ask. How is Marcus working out in the field?"

"He's good, Boss. We're both on the same page when we're neck deep in the shite. He's a man I'd fight side by side with anytime without question."

"Good, good. I was thinking that we might need to get Mr. Harvey back, but if this is working out, then I will leave it at that."

Ilse poked her head through the doorway. "Anja, we've got a hit."

The Talon commander's head snapped around. "Warner?"

"Yes."

"Where?"

"Here in Morocco."

They followed Ilse to where Slania was working on her computer. "Show them, Slania."

She turned the monitor. "This is a café in town ten minutes ago. Sitting out front drinking coffee with Simon Venables."

"Are they still there?" Hawk asked.

"I'm not sure."

"You're not sure?"

Slania shook her head. "No. The cameras in Rabat are shit. One minute they're up, the next nothing. It's like having shit Wi-Fi that drops in and out all the time."

Hawk looked at Anja. "What do you think?"

"I think I want to talk to Mr. Venables. How about you?"

"Let's go."

Anja turned to her deputy. "Ilse, see if you and Slania can set up some kind of satellite link and get eyes on. We'll be on comms."

"Yes, ma'am. We'll do what we can. Do you want Marcus to go with you?"

"No, I think we can handle this."

"YOU'RE ABOUT two minutes out from the café," Slania said.

"How's the uplink coming?" Anja asked.

"Nothing yet. It's like we're suddenly in a dead spot."

"Keep at it."

It was an older part of the city. Hawk slowed down even further to a crawl. The traffic was one way on the narrow street made worse by the pedestrians using it as well. Above them lights hung on wires, spaced out at twenty-foot intervals. As they passed alleys, they could see market stalls packed in side by side servicing a multitude of customers.

"Why couldn't the café be out on the main road somewhere instead of tucked in this rabbit warren?" Hawk growled.

"It adds to the mystique of the city, Jacob," Anja replied.

"I can do without mystique, Boss. It's places like this that are bloody ambush magnets."

"Relax. Turn right up here."

Hawk made the turn and the street widened. Further along was a fountain at the center of a small square.

Anja said, "It should be on the other side of the fountain."

Hawk moved the wheel to go around just as a dark SUV pulled out in front of them and stopped dead. "Shit."

He slammed the Humvee into reverse but went nowhere as another SUV blocked the street. He reached for his Glock and looked out the window to see whether the assailants were on the move. He said, "Alpha Two, we've been boxed in by unknown X-rays. Is that uplink viable yet?"

"Negative, Jake. What's happening?"

"I don't know yet," he said, staring at the vehicle in front of them.

Beside him, Anja had her own weapon out and ready to engage. He felt his pulse quicken as adrenaline kicked in. "Come on, bugger you. Get it started."

The doors opened and four men got out. Three were armed with automatic weapons and wearing body armor and dark shades. The fourth man wore a suit. "Bollocks. That bastard set us up."

"So it would seem, Mr. Hawk. What do we have behind us?"

Hawk looked. "Four more. All dressed like our friends. SAS black ops team."

"Shall we see what he wants?"

"Can I shoot him?"

"No."

"Then I'd rather stay here."

Anja smiled mirthlessly. "Come on, Jake, live a little."

"It's getting harder and harder to do with so much money on my head."

They climbed out and walked to the front of the Humvee. Hawk stared at Venables and said, "You just can't stay away, can you?"

"And you lot keep fucking things up." His voice seethed with anger. "You were told to stay away but here we are again. This time you've gone too far."

"We could say that about you," Anja said.

"Just fucking put them down."

Before they could even move stabbing pains shot through their bodies. Hawk looked down at his side and saw the dart protruding from it. He looked back up at Venables and opened his mouth to speak before everything went dark.

THEY BOTH CAME TO, locked in a cell of an old jail that the black ops team was using as their base of operations. Hawk sat up and looked across at Anja. "Are you all right, Boss?"

She groaned. "I'll live."

"They took our comms and weapons."

"Figures. I wonder where we are."

"Looks like some kind of cell," Hawk said. "I think a more appropriate question is what do they want?"

The cell smelled like old mold, and it made Hawk wonder how long the jail had been out of commission. There were bars on the window, and the walls were made out of red block. On one of the walls, there were tally marks. Made long ago by a prisoner who'd been held there, according to the marks, for ten days.

Hawk pointed them out and said, "I hope we're not in here for that long. I have plans."

Anja nodded. "I have no doubt that we will find out what Mr. Venables wants very shortly."

She pointed at a camera in the corner of the room, its red light flashing, indicating that it was transmitting.

Hawk stood and stretched, then walked over to it and looked up. With a shake of his head, he reached up and ripped it off the wall. "Now that should get his attention."

"Sometimes you can be such a child, Jacob."

"Whatever it takes, Boss."

Within three minutes, the steel door to their cell opened with a loud screech. Two men armed with MP5s walked in, took one look at the prisoners, and the lead one said, "Come with us."

"Where we going?" asked Hawk as though planning his activities around their destination.

"Just move," the SAS Black Ops operator, said.

Hawk looked disappointed but said to him, "I've been

you. Gone down the deep dark rabbit hole, all for the greater good."

"Shut up, asshole."

"Fine. Lead the way. But don't say you weren't warned."

"Warned about what?" the operator asked.

As Hawk walked past him, his right fist bunched, traveled no more than half a foot, with all the force of a horse's kick. The man doubled over in pain while his partner raised his MP5 and pointed it at Hawk's head. "Like I said, you were warned."

At the end of the long dark hallway was a big steel door. Beyond it, in a small block room was a desk. Seated at it was Venables. A typical interrogation scene from an 80's movie with a light bulb hung from a long cord dangling from the ceiling. There must have been a slight breeze in the room somewhere because it slowly wavered from side to side.

There were two vacant chairs. Venables pointed at them both. "Take a seat, and we'll get right down to it."

"You know, you detained us illegally," Anja said.

"I can bloody do anything I like," Venables snarled. "And what's more, I don't give a shit."

"Why are we here?" Anja asked.

"Because you are interfering with an ongoing operation, and quite frankly I've had enough. You will either desist, or I'm going to bury every last one of you in a deep hole where no one will ever find you."

Hawk was suddenly curious. "What operation?"

"We are trying to bring down a terror network. Inside our own country and across Europe," Venables explained. "High profile businessmen who are supplying millions to terror networks across Africa and the Middle East."

"By kidnapping their daughters?" Hawk asked. "Is that it? If you ask me, that's highly fucking illegal. I can't imagine any of your bosses ticking off on something like this."

"My bosses are weak. This is about saving countless lives. We do what must be done."

"So this is so black, so deniable, that they don't even know about it? Is that right?"

"Do not question my motives, Mr. Hawk. What I am doing here is giving you a chance to walk away. Do not think for a moment that should you refuse to take my offer, that you will walk away at all."

Anja leaned forward in her seat. Her eyes narrowed. "Are you threatening us, Mr. Venables?"

"Take it any way you like, Miss Meyer."

"Tell me, what happens to the girls after their fathers are put out of commission, shall we say?"

"Mr. Warner takes care of that issue. Quite frankly, once we have their fathers, I do not care."

Hawk looked at Anja. "Remind me to talk to Warner after we've finished here, Boss."

"I would like to talk to him myself."

Venables sighed. "You are not helping your cause any."

"What happened to Lila Farhadi?"

"It was an accident. The girl struggled, fell and hit her head, and died. There was nothing that could be done."

"An accident that should never have happened," Anja growled, the headache from being drugged intensifying.

"The kidnapping was a means to an end," Venables said tersely. "Do you know what her father does? No? Over the last three years, he has provided over two hundred million dollars to various terrorist groups in North Africa. Farhadi may seem like a family man, but in actual fact, he has sponsored global terrorism. You know that little star you put on your Christmas tree when it comes to holiday time? You know, right at the top? That is Farhadi. He is the pinnacle of the whole network."

"Why not just kill them and be done with it?" Hawk asked. "Leave their daughters out of it."

"Because every one of them will grow up to be like their fathers. You've heard of the black widows, haven't you?"

Hawk nodded. He'd heard of them. When ISIS had come to the fore, and Europeans were flocking to the flag, a group of women banded together. All different nationalities. Slowly they filtered back into Europe and the UK. Over a period of time, female suicide bombers began to appear. Every incident claimed to be the work of the Black Widows. It had taken a nine-month operation to shut down the whole network. In that time, bombs had gone off in eight different countries.

"What you're doing is putting them in the same basket that you've kept the radicals in. Without any evidence."

"I have all the evidence I need."

Suddenly there was an explosion somewhere in the building. Just by the sound, Hawk could easily identify it; an M84 flash bang.

The two armed guards that were in the room with Venables turned to the door, forgetting about their prisoners. Hawk came off his seat and disabled the first one with a kick to the back of a knee and then a chop with the heel of his hand. Then he grabbed a handful of hair and smashed him in the face with a fist.

The second guard made to move, but Anja was too quick for him. She repeated Hawk's actions, working on the back of the knee. Then as the guard went down, she brought up her right foot, kicking him in the side of the head. He was out before he hit the hard concrete floor.

They bent down and picked up the MP5s and then spare ammunition. The sound of gunfire echoed throughout the building and Hawk turned to Venables. "Any idea what's going on?"

"How should I bloody know? I'm in here with you."
The reply was abrupt, angry.

Hawk looked at Anja. "Sounds like a frigging war going on out there."

"Let's just get out of here before we get caught up in it."

Hawk glanced over his shoulder at Venables, gave him a smile. "Be seeing you, you officious prick."

They opened the door and moved out into the hallway. Hawk was on point, the MP5 raised up to his shoulder, ready in case any unfriendly appeared in front of him.

The gunfire grew in intensity. "Someone's having a party."

Suddenly, a masked man dressed in black appeared in front of him. The figure was armed with an AK12. Before Mask could shoot, Hawk stroked the trigger of the MP5 and bullets thundered into the man's chest. He dropped like a stone, the AK-12 clattering to the hard floor.

"I guess we're not getting out of here without a fight, Boss," Hawk said.

At the end of the hallway, they turned to the right, stepping over the corpse of the attacker. Hawk paused and pulled the mask up. The man was middle eastern in appearance, a thin mustache across his top lip. "I wish I had my cell."

Anja took up position covering the approaches. "Check for markings, Jake. See if he has any tattoos."

Hawk did as ordered, and found a small tattoo on the man's right arm. "Crossed Knives."

"I know it. Pakistani Secret Police."

"What the hell are they doing here?"

"I don't think we can ask him at the moment. You can try."

Hawk snorted. "Very funny."

"Follow me. Let's get out of here."

The hallway that they followed opened out into a

84

larger room. It appeared to be what was once the mess for the jail. Now there were three dead men laying on the floor. All were SAS. An attacker appeared to the left through a doorway. Anja fired her weapon and the man jerked and fell. A second shooter appeared behind him and Hawk squeezed the trigger on his own MP5. The attacker buckled at the knees, sank down, and then fell face forward.

The Talon operatives walked swiftly towards the doorway. It led to another hallway which in turn took them to another, larger room. This one had cells on both sides with an open second floor with more of the same.

A shooter appeared above them and opened fire. Bullets cracked into the concrete floor, ricocheting left and right. Anja and Hawk threw themselves sideways. The former SAS operator rolled onto his back, bringing the MP5 around, and squeezed the trigger. Bullets flew upwards like small missiles punching into the shooter's chest. He jerked wildly, falling forward and over the second-floor rail. He hit the concrete floor with a sickening thud, his hooded mask filling with brains as his head split open.

Hawk came to his feet, then hurried across the Anja, who was starting to regain hers. He helped her the rest of the way and said, "This is bullshit, Boss. We need to get out of here before one of these bastards gets lucky. Follow me."

Accessing another steel door brought them out into a large parking lot area. It was overgrown with weeds and vehicle hulks. It also had an intense firefight raging.

Hawk and Anja ducked down behind a wrecked SUV.

Bodies of dead SAS operators lay strewn about the parking lot. Black clad figures had moved fluidly between the wrecked cars, taking them out one at a time. Hawk counted eight men. Anja began rising, ready to fire, but he dragged her back down. "No, we need to get out of here."

He looked around and saw an SUV with its doors open. "Over there."

Keeping low, using the wrecked vehicles for cover, they reached the SUV without incident. Hawk checked and saw that the keys were still in it. "Get in, Boss."

The pair climbed in and the former SAS operator started the motor. He dropped it into gear, popped the clutch, and then spun the wheels as he started to move. Once it was straight, he floored the gas pedal and the SUV shot away, leaving the dead and dying behind them.

Anja looked at Hawk. "What the hell was that?"

"I think we just got caught up in somebody else's war."

"Shit."

"ARE YOU BOTH OKAY?" Ilse asked when they arrived back.

"Only just," Hawk said.

"We had a meeting with our friendly neighborhood MI6 Black Ops director," Anja replied. "Then things went further south when some Pakistani Secret Police showed up and took out the MI6 operation."

"What is Pakistani Secret Police doing here?"

"That is a good question. I needed to talk to Farhadi. Do you have your phone?"

Ilse passed her phone over and Anja took it, walking away so she could make the call. The Talon intel officer looked at Hawk. She reached out and touched his arm. "Are you sure you're okay?"

He leaned in and kissed her. "I'm fine."

Anja was only gone a couple of minutes before returning, a look of concern on her face. "I think we've been played. The phone number I had is disconnected. I have a bad feeling that Farhadi is using us to get to the root of this evil, and now he's capitalized on what we've worked out."

"Have you ever heard the term, 'this just keeps getting better'?" Hawk asked. "Now we've got Pakistani Secret Police added to the mix."

CHAPTER EIGHT

London, England

THE TEAM SPLIT UP. Anja, Slania, and Gray went to London to see what they could find out about Farhadi. Ilse and Hawk went to Sofia, Bulgaria, based on a thin lead found by Slania. One which linked Warner with a known sex trafficker named Kosta Kalchev. They took a punt on the fact that if Warner were selling the girls after they'd been used, then this would be the location.

In the meantime, Anja and the others were trying to piece the London end together.

"My name is Anja Meyer, I'm here to see Mr. Farhadi."

The woman behind the counter stared at the three of them and said, "I'm sorry, Mr. Farhadi isn't in."

"Are you sure?"

"Of course. He hasn't been in for the past few days."

"Do you mind if we check for ourselves?" Anja asked.

"I already told you—wait, where are you going?"

The three Talon people had already turned away and were walking towards the bank of elevators. The flustered receptionist waved frantically at a security guard.

He stepped away from the wall where he was posted and moved to block their way. "I'm sorry, folks but—"

That was a far as he got. A few fast moves from Gray and he was unconscious on the floor. The former para turned back to the receptionist and said, "He'll be all right. Just have a slight headache, that's all."

"I would have killed him," Slania said in a low voice.

They climbed in the elevator car when it arrived and went up to the floor where Farhadi's office was located. Except it wasn't. There was no one there at all.

"It all smells a little fishy to me," Gray said in a mock voice.

"We've been bloody had," Anja growled. "When I get my hands on him, I'm going to put a nine-millimeter slug in his fucking head."

They returned to the lobby and walked up to the reception desk. The receptionist saw them coming and took a step back. Anja leaned on the counter. "Where is he?"

"I—I don't know."

"He just cleaned everything out and you don't know where he went?"

"He never said."

"I need his home address."

"I—I can't—"

Anja leaned closer. "Now."

"S—sure." She scribbled it down on a piece of paper and slid it across the desk. "Here."

"Thank you."

And with that, they walked out of the building and straight into trouble.

———

THERE WERE MAYBE twenty armed police from the Specialist Firearms Command or SCO19. All had weapons pointed at them ready to fire. Gray turned to Anja and said, "This doesn't look too good."

Like Moses parting the Red Sea, the officers moved back in what appeared to be a choreographed move, revealing a very live Simon Venable. "You are under arrest for aiding and abetting in the escape of a known terrorist."

"Take it easy, Simon," a second man said as he moved through the cordon of armed men. "This is Five's jurisdiction."

"No, Frank. They got good men killed. They belong to Six. I mean to have them."

Frank Fitzgerald shook his head. "You know better than that, Simon."

"We'll see. I'll kick it up to the Home Secretary and we'll see what unfolds."

"You do that, but I will have them."

Venables stomped off, leaving Fitzgerald standing in front of the guns. The MI5 chief stepped forward. He was somewhere between the age of 50 and 60 and it was catching up with his face. "Hello, Anja."

"Frank."

"It seems you've gotten yourself into a bit of a fix."

She nodded. "We're used to it."

"I have a car waiting. Ride with me. The others can ride with a marked unit."

"Where are we going?" Anja asked.

"Back to Five."

Anja looked at the others. "You'll be fine. I trust Frank."

"You sure, Boss?" Gray asked.

"Yes, quite sure."

"All right then."

Fitzgerald escorted Anja over to what had once been a Black Cab, now an armored vehicle which transported Fitzgerald wherever he went. They climbed in and the driver pulled out into the flow of traffic.

"Where is that rascal you usually have tagging along?"

"Looking into something for me with my intel officer."

"Shame. I rather think he's quite capable."

"That's why he is doing what he is."

The ride took twenty minutes. Ten minutes after that, Anja was in Fitzgerald's office. "Would you like to start with what happened in Morocco?"

"Venables took Jake and I off the street. It was a setup. He and his team were operating out of some abandoned jail. While we were there, former Pakistani Secret Police raided the place and shot the shit out of his team. I actually thought he was dead as well. As you can see, no such luck."

"Why are you here in London?"

"I wanted to question Farhadi. I believe that the Pakistani soldiers are his. Hired mercenaries."

"You're sure they're from Pakistan?"

"Yes."

"Interesting."

Anja nodded. "So was the fact that Farhadi is gone."

"Quite. Now, about these allegations of you and yours interfering in a Six operation."

"I guess in a way we were, Frank," Anja admitted. "But Venables was so far out of his lane it wasn't funny. Do you have any idea what they were doing?"

"It is a need-to-know op," Fitzgerald said.

"They kidnapped young women to get to their fathers. Killed their fathers and then made the women disappear," Anja hissed.

The MI6 commander frowned. "Are you saying they were killed, Anja?"

"No, I think they were sold, trafficked by Brian Warner. The latest one was supposed to be Doctor Kaaya Ismat. She is in protective custody."

"The daughter of Jaalib Ismat?"

"Yes."

"Bloody hell. We just concluded an investigation into him. He's clean. There's nothing to the rumors."

"Then you need to protect him before Venables kills him."

Fitzgerald reached for the phone and made the call.

When he replaced the receiver, Fitzgerald said, "Now, let's get back to this Six issue. The truth is, I'm probably not going to be able to hold them off for long. Tell me what you need."

"To speak to Farhadi's wife and then to get out of the country where I can find Farhadi himself. He's the only one who can clear this mess up."

"I'll get you some transport so you can go see the woman. Then get to your plane. Don't dally, Anja. Six plays nasty when they feel they've been slighted."

"Thank you, Frank."

"Don't let me down."

NOBODY ANSWERED THE DOOR. They knocked four times but all they got was silence. Anja turned to Gray and said, "Marcus, find me a way in."

In true British eloquence, Gray took out his handgun and shot the lock.

The house was more of a stone mansion set on two acres surrounded by a large fence and evergreen hedges. The gardens were well maintained and the lawns manicured; there was a small lake at the bottom corner.

Once inside, they found emptiness. The house, like the office, had been totally cleaned out. Anja said, "Spread out, look around."

They went from room to room looking for anything which might help. In the end it was Gray who found the secret room in the study.

It was like a James Bond film in which a secret lever

opens a door. The former para was looking around when he noticed the faint scratches on the polished hardwood floor. Not straight, which might occur naturally moving furniture, but curved.

And, as in the movies, all roads lead to Rome. He stepped up to the empty bookcase and tried to move it. It was fixed. He looked around thinking there might be something visible. Then he saw the small button on the side, not unlike a cap placed over a screw to cover it. Gray pressed it, the latch snicked, and the bookcase moved.

"Well now, what do we have here?"

He swung the hidden door open, and it revealed a room. "Bingo."

Sofia, Bulgaria

Hawk walked into the bar with Ilse and stopped. Doing a quick scan of all the patrons, he moved his assessment to the bar itself.

"Do you see him?" Ilse asked.

"I'm not even sure he still owns it," Hawk replied.

He looked around some more, the watched becoming the watchers as heads started to turn in their direction. Ilse said, "Let's get a drink. We're beginning to draw attention."

They walked across the room to the bar and ordered two beers from a thin blonde woman wearing an apron. It was then that Hawk noticed the beer coasters. They all had the British flag printed on them. He stopped the waitress before she could walk away. "Lass, where can I find Whitey Fisher?"

"Who?" She looked confused.

"Robert?"

"Oh, I get for you."

She disappeared while Hawk and Ilse found a table to sit at. Ilse said, "You know this man from the Regiment?"

"That's right. We served a while together before he got out. He married a girl from Bulgaria. They stayed in London for a while but then moved here. He—"

"Jacob fucking Hawk, as I live and breathe."

Hawk looked up at the large man, a mass of red hair and beard coming towards their table. The former SAS operator stood up and extended his hand. Fisher batted it away and wrapped his arms around him in a bear hug. "Piss off. Is that any way to greet an old mucker?"

"Good to see you, Whitey," Hawk said.

"You, too."

Hawk pointed at Ilse. "Mate, this is Ilse Geller. We work together."

Fisher smiled at her. "Pleased to meet you, lass. I hope you're keeping this scouser under control?"

"You know Jake, it's impossible," Ilse replied.

He nodded. "Yeah, that's about it. Anyhow, why don't I get myself a beer and we can chat."

Fisher went over to the bar and got himself a beer. Ilse leaned across the table and said to Hawk, "He is big."

"That he is. I've seen him take two bullets and fight all day before he left the battlefield."

She gave him a doubtful look. "Jacob, really."

"All right, it was three hours, but he did it."

Fisher came back and sat down. "What can I do for you, Jake? I'm guessing that this isn't a social visit."

Hawk shook his head. "Sorry, Mucker, it's not. I need some information."

"I'll try to help."

"Have you had any interesting customers lately?"

"Mate, it's a pub. We get nothing but interesting customers. You'll have to be more specific."

"Former military. Mercs even."

"Maybe a few."

94

"Recently?"

"Mucker, just stick your dick in all the way instead of poking at it." He glanced at Ilse. "Sorry."

"Brian Warner. We heard he was here possibly meeting with Kosta Kalchev."

"Wow, Jake, still pissing in the big boys' pool, huh?"

"Comes with the job."

"Kalchev is the big cheese around Sofia, Jake," Fisher explained. "He cuts the balls off people he likes just for fun. You should see what he does to those he doesn't like."

"We're trying to find some kidnapped girls. If we can find Warner, we are hoping he will lead us to the girls."

"Just the two of you?" Fisher asked incredulously.

"That's right."

"I should tell you all I know, Jake. You deserve to get killed for being so stupid."

"Now you're just calling me names for the hell of it, Whitey."

The pub owner stroked his beard. "Shit. All right, I'll start with Kalchev. The prick runs all the street walkers, knock shops, and strip clubs in Sofia. The bastard is worth a packet. The street walkers are under the watchful eye of Nayden Ivkov. The prick is a hardnosed asshole who runs the girls with an iron fist. They screw up, he beats the shit out of them. They do it again and they are found dead in the gutter. He feeds them cocaine to keep them under control."

"Sounds nice."

"They say he used to be Bulgarian Secret Police."

"I thought they were disbanded in eighty-nine," Ilse said.

"Officially they were. But they were closely allied to the Russian KGB of the time. All they did was go underground. They're still out there, you just can't see them."

"The world is full of secrets," Hawk said. "Tell us more."

"The knock shops—"

"The what?" Ilse asked.

"Brothels," Fisher said.

"Oh."

"The brothels are run by Lassen Petkov. He's not as bad as Ivkov but he's still a nasty bugger."

"If these girls were here, where would they be?" Hawk asked.

Fisher shook his head. Hawk could tell it pained the man to even speak about it. "When the girls first arrive, they are taken to the coke farm. They lock them up there while feeding them cocaine until they're hooked before turning them loose."

"Bastards."

"Even the prostitutes at the brothels are coke addicted."

Hawk nodded. "But where might I find them?"

Fisher drank some of his beer. He wiped his mouth then shrugged. "Depends. What kind of girls are we talking about?"

"Middle Eastern heritage," Ilse said.

"The streets. Kalchev fought in the Afghan War with the Soviets. He hates anyone like that with a passion. You'll find your girls on the streets."

"Where is the coke farm?"

"Stay away from it, Jake. You'll only find death there."

"Can't do it, Whitey. I need to find this girl. From what I can work out, that's where she'll be."

"You're a crazy bastard, Jake."

Hawk grinned at him. "I had a good teacher. You know where I can get some guns?"

———

"Have you found anything?" Anja asked Slania and Gray.

Gray said, "Just papers that don't mean shit to me."

"I have something," Slania said. She held up three pieces of paper. "These are documents outlining donations to charities in the Middle East and North Africa. I'm reasonably sure that I recognize at least two names that are covers for terror organizations."

"Take them."

Gray opened a drawer and found more paperwork. Then, hiding in the back, he found a ledger. He took it out and opened it. It was like finding a gold mine. As his eyes looked at the writing, he could tell what it was. "Boss, you're going to want to see this."

Anja crossed to where he was standing and he passed her the book. Anja flicked through it and looked up at Gray. "This is everything we need. It's time to go."

"There's still one more drawer over here," Gray said and pulled it open.

There was an audible click followed by a beeping sound. Anja looked at him as he went deathly quiet. "Marcus, what did you do?"

"I'll tell you after we get out of here. Run!"

The timer read ten seconds. They hadn't even reached the front door when the first charge blew. By the time the second went, they were almost there. The third shoved them out the door.

All three Talon people crashed to the turn around when the fourth charge blew, bringing the roof down. Orange flame and black smoke billowed up into the leaden sky. Anja rolled onto her back and sat up, pain coursing through her body. She looked at the burning building and said, "Are you two all right?"

"I'm good, Boss," said Gray.

"Me, too," Slania said with a groan.

Anja said, "He knew we would come. That's why he rigged the house."

Gray nodded. "He did, at that. But there is one thing he overlooked, the fact that we might get away from the blast."

The sound of revving engines reached out to them where they sat. And before long two black SUVs appeared in the driveway. Anja said, "No, he didn't. Into the gardens, now."

———

THE SOUND of machine gun fire was hot on their heels as they sprinted away. Bullets kicked up at their feet, chasing them out of sight. The gardens and lawns were well looked after, the beds themselves well defined. The path they were on split into three and they each took a different route. Anja said, "Remember, these people are good at what they do. Be better."

Slania drew her Glock and moved off the path into a garden with dense foliage. She disappeared inside and found that beyond the green wall of outer foliage was an open area. Standing just beyond the edge she watched two masked shooters, armed with AK-12s, go past. The third seemed to have some sixth sense that someone was watching. He looked straight at Slania and the tech held her breath wondering if he could see her.

The masked shooter left the path and walked towards her position. He paused for a moment and looked down. There in a bare patch of earth at the edge of the garden was a clear boot print.

The shooter scanned the bushes before him and raised his weapon to his shoulder. His intent to fire was etched in his face but before he could squeeze the trigger, Slania fired the Glock twice and put him down.

Then she turned and moved deeper into the thick bushes before the others came back.

———

GRAY HEARD the shots and hesitated. He waited for more to ring out, but they never came. He heard the approach of someone behind him and he left the path to hide behind a large oak. He waited patiently until two masked shooters appeared. As they traversed the path he circled the tree, keeping its large trunk between himself and them.

However, once they were past, Gray stepped out, raised the Glock, and opened fire.

The first shooter went down with two bullets in his back, thrust forward by an unseen hand. The second shooter spun swiftly around, bringing his AK-12 into play. His problem was that he was too quick on the trigger and even before he was completely turned, he was already wildly spraying bullets.

Gray dropped to a knee and fired again. The bullet punched into the shooter's side as he was turning. The former para fired twice more. Once at the chest, then again at the head. The third round entered the killer's open mouth as he was screaming. The slug smashed teeth before blowing through the spine and out at the base of the killer's neck.

Elsewhere nearby, Gray could hear gunfire, so he slipped deeper into the garden.

———

ANJA RELOADED as she lay behind a stone fountain. Bullets blew chips off the carvings and howled off into the undergrowth. She slapped the magazine home and opened fire again. A shooter with an automatic weapon fell to the ground, but there were two remaining.

They unloaded a withering burst of fire in Anja's direction and soon she was pinned down. "Well done," she admonished herself.

Another fusillade of shots reached her ears. These were much sharper. The gunfire in her direction halted and she looked over the edge of the fountain. There she saw Gray and Slania coming towards her. Gray said, "Come on, Boss, we need to get out of here."

Anja came to her feet and said, "We need to get out of the country."

Over the English Channel

"Where are we headed to, Boss?" Gray asked Anja.

"Bulgaria, where we can sift through this intel and help out Jake and Ilse to wrap up what they're doing."

Slania looked up from her computer. "There is a lot of good stuff here. Farhadi was making donations to different charities across the globe. All of them were fronts for terror organizations."

"Is there any indication as to where he might have gone?" Anja asked her.

"No." She glanced back at her screen to make sure there was nothing she'd missed.

"Keep looking. We need him to clear us of any wrong-doing. What about Warner?"

"He's gone to ground. I can't—hold on."

"What is it?"

"There's been an incident in Amsterdam," Slania explained.

"What kind of incident?"

"A shootout between what they're calling Muslim extremists and a local gang."

Anja nodded. "It looks like Farhadi found him before we did. Any figures?"

"A few dead on both sides but after the fight was over, the survivors disappeared."

"That's it, then," said Anja. "We're going to Amsterdam."

CHAPTER NINE

Sofia, Bulgaria

THREE PROSTITUTES STOOD TOGETHER on a corner talking, smoking cigarettes. Hawk guessed they were ready for another hit of cocaine and used the nicotine to try and take the edge off the cravings. He and Ilse had been watching them for the past hour to get the lay of the land.

Every now and then one more would appear, dropped off by a vehicle before another vehicle stopped to pick up a girl in a constant revolving door of sex for sale.

"I can't figure out how humans can exploit one another like this, Jake," Ilse said. "I truly can't."

"Money and greed," he replied simply.

"I can't see Ivkov anywhere."

"He won't be far away. Or at least someone with a link to him."

"What are we going to do?"

Hawk reached into the rear seat of the SUV and grabbed the MP5. "Take this."

"Where are you going?"

"To ask some questions."

"Be careful."

Stuffing the Glock 17 that Fisher had given him into his pants, Hawk climbed from the BMW X5 and started across the street.

The girls were young and hopped up on coke. It wasn't hard to tell. He glanced at their arms and could see the tracks. Hawk felt his guts turn over and wished Ivkov was there so he could shoot him in the face.

"What you want, baby?" one of the girls asked. It sounded like Russian.

"English," Hawk said, tapping his chest.

The girl looked at her friends. Another, a dark-haired girl with black rings around her eyes stepped forward and said in halting English, "You want suck dick or fuck, English?"

"Where?" Hawk asked.

She pointed to an alley. "There."

Hawk nodded. "Sure, why not."

He followed her towards the alley and once they turned the corner into the narrow thoroughfare, she stopped and turned toward him. Fumbling with his fly, she slurred, "You have large dick, big boy? Fill my mouth?"

"Wait," he said.

She looked up at his face with bleary eyes. "You want fuck me then?"

"No. I want to ask you a couple of questions."

She stepped back. "No."

Hawk grabbed her arm. "I'll pay you double."

"What is problem?" a man said from behind them.

The guy must have been hiding in the shadows. Hawk turned. "No problem, mate. We're just discussing price."

"No discuss. Fuck then leave."

Hawk walked over to him. "It's all right, mate. I'll do just that."

"No, Boris, he want to ask questions."

103

It was evident that she was fearful of the man, which was why she blurted the truth. She knew what would happen if she lied and he found out. Which put Hawk in a situation.

"What?" The man reached for a weapon hidden under his coat.

Hawk's right fist shot out and found his jaw. The man staggered backward, his arms windmilling as he tried to regain his balance. While he was doing that, Hawk grabbed his shoulder and spun him. His right arm looped around the man's neck and his left completed the hold. The Brit squeezed tightly, whispering in the man's ear, "Don't fight it, mate. Just relax."

Moments later the man blacked out, dropping to the ground as Hawk released him.

Stepping away from the prone form, Hawk looked over at the girl who was backing away. He lunged forward and caught her arm again.

"Let me go!" Her entreaty was accompanied by a vicious shake, trying to dislodge her captor.

"In a moment. Just be still. Have you seen this girl?" Releasing her arm, he made sure she wasn't going to bolt, then retrieved a photo of Heba Hassan from his pocket. He held it out to her.

She gave it a cursory glance before replying, "No."

He put the picture back and took out another. "What about this one?"

He could tell by her expression she was about to lie. "No."

"I know you are lying. Where is she?"

"She—she is dead." The girl looked down at the rough surface of the alley and shuffled her feet.

"How?" Hawk asked, lifting her chin to make her look at him so that he could identify if she was telling the truth.

"An overdose."

"Where is Ivkov?"

"I—I don't know."

"Where?"

"Maybe the café," she replied hesitantly.

"Where is the café?"

"Across the street." She indicated with a nod of her head.

"Thank you," Hawk said and took out some money. "Here, get clean, and go home."

She hung her head in shame. "I cannot."

"Suit yourself," Hawk replied and turned away.

"Where you go?"

"To kill a man," he replied.

———

ILSE FELT on edge when she saw the man disappear into the alley after Hawk and the prostitute. She gripped the MP5 a little tighter and her breath quickened. When nothing happened, she relaxed a little. Then Hawk appeared from the alley mouth and started across the street towards the café.

"What are you doing, Jake?" she whispered to herself.

He kept walking.

Ilse climbed from the SUV and moved to stand by the hood. He saw her and said, "Stay there. I'll be out in a moment."

"Jake, what are you doing?" she asked him cautiously.

"Just get in the Beamer and start the motor. I'll be right back."

Ilse knew that whatever he was up to, wasn't good. "You're not going to do something stupid, are you?"

"I might," he replied as he stepped up onto the sidewalk.

Ilse grabbed the MP5 tighter and climbed into the BMW. "Give me strength."

THE BELL RANG as Hawk opened the door to the café. It had one of those annoying, high-pitched jingles that announced to everyone, "Hey, here I am."

Every diner within the establishment turned their head to look at him. All five of them. Covered in tatts, some piercings, all armed with some form of weapon.

Hawk picked Ivkov out right away. The one at the rear table with his back to the wall so he could see who was coming and going. There were two others with him.

There seemed to be only two options open to Hawk. He could talk to the man, then kill him, or the more sensible route was to just start shooting and see what happened.

As fond as he was of a good firefight, he chose the former.

As he walked up to Ivkov's table, one of the thugs looked at him disdainfully and asked, "What the fuck you want?"

Taking the pictures from his pocket once more, Hawk threw them on the table. "I'm looking for these girls. I know one of them is dead. What about the others?"

Ivkov looked disinterestedly at the pictures, hawked, and then spit on them. He gave the Talon operative a look of contempt and said, "Fuck off."

"If that's the way you want it," Hawk said and pulled the Glock.

Aim and fire. Three times. The thug on Ivkov's right died with his brains splattered on the wall behind him. The same with the one on his left. Ivkov, however, was incapacitated with a shot to his chest. He would live long enough for Hawk to question while he dealt with the remaining two.

Hawk turned and fired at the other thugs who lurched from their chairs, desperately grabbing for their weapons.

BANG! BANG! Both down.

Hawk moved back to the table where Ivkov was hunched over. Hawk lifted his head by a handful of hair and looked at his pain filled face, blood starting to run from the corner of his mouth.

"Looks like I clipped a lung there, Nayden," Hawk said. "Oh well, a doctor might save you. But while you wait, tell me about the girls."

He tried to speak but nothing came out.

"What was that? I didn't quite hear."

"H—house."

"The house? What house?"

"Drug."

"Thanks," Hawk said and shot him in the head.

Returning to the front door of the diner, he checked the room once more, then pushed through and stepped onto the sidewalk. Ilse pulled up in the BMW, and he climbed in.

She looked at him. "That was stupid, Jake."

"Made me feel better, and I found out she's at the drug house."

"Did you find out where it was?" she asked, a little more than pissed.

He stared straight ahead as they drove along the street. "Maybe not."

"Shit."

———

Amsterdam, Netherlands

Landing at a private airport on the outskirts of Amsterdam, the team were met by an old friend of Anja's from German intelligence who had organized their access to the airfield. Harald Graf had been Anja's mentor when she'd first started out.

He stepped forward and kissed her on both cheeks. "Anja, my dear, it is good to see you."

She smiled at him. "You, too, Harald. I can't thank you enough for what you have done."

He looked at the others.

Anja said, "These are my colleagues. Marcus Gray and Slania Albring. This is Harald Graf, an old friend."

Graf stepped forward and shook hands with Gray. "Pleased to meet you."

"You, too, sir."

He turned to face Slania. "And you, my dear."

His hand extended. "I don't touch," Slania said unapologetically.

Graf nodded. "It seems I remember someone else like that. Where is Karl?"

An uncomfortable silence fell over the group until Anja broke it. "I'm afraid Karl was killed."

"Oh, dear. I always liked him. I'm so sorry." He pointed at two awaiting SUVs. "Ride with me. The others will come along in the second. Your pilots will be taken care of."

"Thank you, Harald."

They climbed into the SUVs and the drivers pulled away. Harald looked at Anja, a satisfied expression on his face. "I have been following your progress, Anja. You and your people have done great work. Achieved something none of us had been able to when you stopped Medusa."

"Thank you, Harald. It came at a cost. But I'm afraid all it did was leave a vacuum to be filled."

"I don't think you fully understand just what you did, my dear. Now, what can I help you with?"

"Are you familiar with the shootout yesterday?"

"Yes."

"It wasn't gangs, was it?"

He stared at her. "Why do I get the feeling that you already know more about this than what you are telling?"

"We believe that it was a fight between Brian Warner and men recruited by Akmal Farhadi."

"Uh huh. Big players."

Anja looked exasperated. "Why am I the last frigging person to find this shit out?"

Graf grabbed her hand. "Take a breath. Then tell me about it."

"We were hired to look into a kidnapping. Lila Farhadi. She was killed in the process."

"Oh, dear."

"We decided to take it on for the very reason that it seemed as though it were part of a sex trafficking operation, and we needed to shut it down."

"I see."

Anja continued. "We stumbled across an MI6 Deep Black operation run by an agent named Simon Venables. They were using Warner to kidnap the daughters to get to the supposed terrorist-sponsoring fathers. They're a damn execution squad."

"What happens to the girls?" Graf asked.

"Warner has been selling them to Kosta Kalchev."

The German shook his head. "Not a good outcome."

"The worst. But as usual, there is more. Farhadi was using us to find those responsible so he could exact revenge upon them. Well, Farhadi tracked down Venables and his SAS unit. Then Venables screamed that we were involved, and now we're wanted by MI6."

"I had seen the memo."

"Add to that, one of my people has a twenty-million bounty on his head."

"Oh, yes, the unconventional Jacob Hawk."

"I would call him a lot of things, but unconventional would be further down the list."

Graf smiled. "You always attracted the strong ones."

"Something like that."

A sigh came from Graf and he said, "The police only

released some of the information. The intelligence agencies have their own sources. The Muslim terrorists were former Pakistani Special Forces."

"Definitely Farhadi. We've run across them before."

"And the others were mercenaries. We managed to get some footage and, even though it's grainy, it looks like they were after Warner."

"So, he is here," Anja said.

"Is, was. It's hard to tell if he still is."

"What about Farhadi's men?"

"They've disappeared like Warner and his. Although there might be a thread you can pull on."

"We're quite adept at pulling on strings. Who might we find at the end of this one?"

"Liv Faas."

"Who is Liv Faas?" Anja asked.

"She operates a sex ring within Amsterdam. Buys girls from whoever she can now, ever since you took down Medusa."

"Why hasn't she been put out of business?" Anja asked.

Graf shrugged. "Money talks. She has more than one politician in her pocket."

"Where are we going now?"

"I have a safe place for you to stay. Everything you need to know about the woman will be there. That way, tonight you can go and have a little talk to her."

"What about weapons? Things like that?" Anja asked.

"My dear, you will find everything there that you require."

"Thank you, Harald."

———

THE RESIDENCE they were supplied was a terrace house, overlooking a busy street. The first thing that Gray did when they arrived was make sure there was more than one exit point. Inside, in a duffel bag, they found weapons. Three MP5SDs along with Glock handguns. Beside the bag lay a folder. Anja opened it and started to flick through all the papers and photos within.

Liv Faas, the daughter of a Dutch millionaire, had inherited her father's business portfolio upon his sudden death a couple of years earlier. But business was slow, with a downturn in the market, so she'd turned to alternative ways to supplement her income.

Right across Amsterdam, she now owned numerous brothels and strip clubs. But prostitution wasn't the only thing she ran from her night clubs. Amsterdam was in the grip of an ecstasy pandemic, the source of which could be traced back to Liv Faas.

Slania picked up a photo and stared at it. The woman could almost have been a fashion model; her features fine, her hair long and dark, her body slim and attractive. That's if you liked killers. German intelligence had linked her to at least seven deaths in the past two years. Slania said, "She's pretty hot for a killer."

"Does she take your fancy?" asked Gray.

Slania grinned at him. "I don't mind my bread buttered on both sides."

"There you go. You learn something every day." Gray started to pick through the papers himself. "I wonder what sort of security team she runs."

Anja passed him a photo. "A close support team of three by the looks of this. Judging by the photo, I'd say they were ex-military. Hell, everyone is ex-military."

"It will be tough getting close to her," Gray observed, placing a photo back on the table.

Slania said, "If we could separate them from her, then we might be in with a show."

"Yes, but how do we do that?"

Anja stared at the photo. "A woman like that wouldn't

drive herself. She'd have her own car set up. Possibly a black SUV, armored."

"You sound like you're already putting together a plan, Boss," Gray said.

"Maybe, Marcus. Just maybe. Slania, dig deeper. I want to know what vehicle she has, where she parks it, and how far away it is. We'll have one shot at this, and I want it done fast and successfully."

"What rules of engagement are we going to operate by, Boss?" Gray asked.

"We shoot them if they shoot at us. If not, I don't want to draw too much unwanted attention."

"Understood."

———

"IS EVERYONE IN POSITION?" Anja asked.

"Roger that."

"Go covert."

All three pulled their masks over their faces and prepared for what came next.

"Target moving," Slania said over their comms.

"Target vehicle in sight," Gray said. "All clear."

Gray caught movement in the parking garage then he saw them. "Going loud."

"Moving," Anja said.

Gray pulled the pin on the stun grenade and threw it across the concrete towards the approaching figures. Moments later it detonated.

The four figures reeled from the blast, staggering around. Gray and Anja moved swiftly from two different sides. The former para put the first man down with a blow from his weapon, followed by the second as well. The third began to recover but Gray took him out at the knees with a swift kick. The man cried out in pain as he fell, but the Brit silenced it with another solid hit.

In the time it took him to put down the three guards, Anja had Faas trussed up, hood over her head, and ready for transport.

Gray went through the guards' pockets looking for keys. He found a fob and pressed the button. With a beep and flash of indicators they had their ride pinpointed. "There."

They hustled Faas towards it and shoved her into the rear seat. Anja climbed in beside her and pushed her down. "Stay there."

On the way out of the garage, Gray stopped and Slania climbed in. "Looks all clear," she said.

"Good. Bravo Two, take us somewhere quiet."

"Who are you?" Faas asked, her voice muffled through the hood.

"Shut up and stay quiet," Anja hissed.

Gray drove through the streets until he reached the industrial area. He found a rundown warehouse and stopped. Slania climbed out and opened the large sliding door. It rumbled on rollers, screeching in protest as it went.

Gray drove inside and stopped. Behind the SUV, Slania closed the door.

Anja opened her door and dragged Faas roughly from the vehicle. The warehouse had been scouted beforehand and a chair placed in the middle of the concrete floor. Faas was tied to it while Gray turned on the flood lights.

When everything was ready, Anja ripped the hood from their prisoner's head. She blinked rapidly against the bright lights. "What do you want?"

"Answer a couple of questions and we shall let you go," Anja replied. "It is that simple."

"What questions?"

"We're looking for Brian Warner."

"I do not know any Brian Warner."

"But you do. I know you do. He's your go-to man when buying your girls."

Her eyes flared.

Anja continued. "Don't worry about them. As of right now, you are out of business. Every single club, brothel, anything that you've touched is shut down."

"Who are you?"

Anja removed her mask. "We're Talon."

"The ones who stopped Medusa?"

"That's right."

Faas remained silent.

"Where is Warner?"

"I do not know."

"We can protect you," Anja told her.

"From who?" Faas asked. "I do not need protecting."

"From Akmal Farhadi. He wants Warner and everyone else connected to the death of his daughter."

"I had nothing to do with her death. I don't even know her."

Anja said, "That won't matter. Akmal is after Warner. You have a relationship with Warner. He will come and extract all he can from you, and when he is finished, he might give you to his men to play with before they kill you."

Anja didn't know if the last part was true, but it sounded convincing.

It seemed so to Faas as well. "I do not know exactly where he is. It might have changed after what happened."

"The gun fight?"

"Yes. He was staying at one of his houses outside of Amsterdam, but I would say he has moved."

"To where?"

"There is an abandoned coal mine outside of Amsterdam. He could have gone there," Faas explained.

"How do you contact him?" Anja asked.

"I cannot. I have tried."

"Then we'd better check out the—"

"We've got incoming, Boss," Slania interrupted.

"Marcus," Anja snapped as she started to untie Faas.

"On it, Boss."

Gray grabbed his MP5SD and ran towards the front door of the warehouse. Opening it slightly, he saw two SUVs pulling up and six armed men dressed in black climbing out. They looked to have SIG SG 550s. "Shit."

He ran back to the vehicle. "No time, Boss. We have to make a stand."

Slania checked her weapon, making sure there was a round ready to go. Anja said, "Has everyone got their suits on?"

"Roger that."

They slipped into their body armor and prepared. Anja said, "The only cover we have is the SUV."

"It's armored so it will be good. We just have to wait for them to get inside."

Slania hurried over to the lights and started shining them towards the door. "This should help."

"Good idea."

With that done, and Faas shoved back into the rear of the SUV, the team waited for the intruders to arrive.

CHAPTER TEN

Amsterdam, Netherlands

THEY CAME in with a military precision instilled over a long period of time. They all went left or right, covering their space.

Gray leaned out from behind the vehicle with his MP5SD and opened fire. The burst was short, but the shooter went down hard. His companions were startled by the ferocity of the unexpected attack, and they started spraying bullets wildly in his direction.

Their carelessness opened the door for Anja and Slania who fired their own guns, dropping an additional two shooters. After only seconds the attackers had lost half of their force.

Gray hunkered down as bullets hammered the armored SUV. He waited until it lessened and rose to his feet to fire, but was forced back to cover by heavily intensified gunfire, before he could take a shot.

Then came an explosion. One of the attackers had thrown a stun grenade which exploded behind the three Talon operatives.

Ears rang and brains were rattled. Gray seemed to fall on his side, his vision blurred. The former para blinked his eyes to clear the fog away. Then as they came back into focus, through the gap underneath the vehicle, he saw feet running towards the SUV.

Gray squeezed the trigger and saw bullets strike the legs, knocking them from beneath the shooter.

As the man hit the hard concrete, a cry of pain exploded from his mouth. Gray shifted his aim and shot him in the head.

That left two.

Beside him, Slania had regained her composure, thanks to her training. She turned and fired dangerously over the top of Gray at a shooter who appeared around the end of the vehicle. The man fell, his weapon clattering to the ground.

Anja claimed the last shooter. He was taken by a single shot to the head from her handgun as her came around the front of the SUV. No fuss, just a steady hand.

"Clear!" Gray shouted.

"Clear!" Slania concurred.

"Check our package," Anja said.

"Roger," Slania replied.

Faas lay shaking on the rear seat, alive, but scared.

"The package is fine," Slania said.

"Good. Let's get some pictures and leave before more turn up."

Three minutes later they were mobile again. "Where to, Boss?" Gray asked.

"I know of a place. We will lay low there and set up surveillance on the address that Faas here will give us. Once we have it, she will make a stop at the Interpol office."

"No," she gasped, fear in her tone.

"Yes, you have a lot to answer for. Or if you prefer, I

117

can kick you out here and you can take your chances with Farhadi's men."

She harrumphed and crossed her arms.

"I thought so."

———

London, England

"Things are starting to get out of control, Simon. You need to rein them in," the man sitting across the table in the private lounge said to Venables. He took a sip of his whiskey and said, "People are starting to notice."

Venables knocked the ash off the cigar he'd been chewing on and said, "It is Talon, Michael. They're getting too big for their boots."

"Then do something about them."

"I'm trying, believe me."

"I can't have them stopping the operation before it is complete."

"I understand, Michael."

The man named Michael took a pull at his own cigar and then swiped some ash off his suit jacket. He exhaled a cloud of blue-gray smoke and said, "Do you know where Farhadi has absconded to?"

"No. He has declared war on me and my section, however. He will show again."

"I thought that was Talon who killed your people?" Michael questioned.

"No, it was Farhadi. I used that story to slow them down."

Michael nodded. "Good thinking. Now, about your friend, Warner."

"What about him?"

"I want him disposed of. This all started because of him. There should be consequences."

Venables nodded. "He's in Amsterdam. I can have a black team there in a few hours."

"And Jaalib Ismat?"

"If we move on him now, it won't be made look like a heart attack," Venables pointed out. "He is under protection, and we don't have his daughter."

"I think we're beyond that, Simon. Speed things up."

"All right."

Michael took another sip of his whiskey and watched the liquid run back into the bottom of the glass. "We'll teach these bastards that it doesn't pay to make an enemy of Michael Bennett."

———

IT WAS dark and wet when they came for Jaalib Ismat. MI5 had sequestered him and his wife in a small terrace in the middle of London under the watchful eye of one team. Two members in a van outside were running surveillance, while two more were in the home.

Ismat was drinking coffee while reading the morning's newspaper left on the sofa by one of the other agents. The front page was a large picture of the latest British PM to have been ousted by his colleagues for being unlikable or some shit like that. In the Middle East a terror group had blown up an oil well while Somali pirates were back at their games off the coast of Africa.

Ismat went to the sport section to see that the T20 World Cup Cricket had started in Australia and that England had won their first match against New Zealand.

Concentrating on the paper, he tipped his coffee cup a little too far while taking a sip, a runnel of coffee splashing down his cheek and onto the end of his chin. He swiped it with his hand before it could stain his shirt. "Bastard."

Grover, the MI5 agent, looked up from the book he was reading. "Is everything all right?"

"Trying to spill my coffee," Ismat explained.

Grover nodded and picked up his own cup to take a sip. He placed it back on the small table and nodded. "You don't make a bad cup, Jaalib."

"It is all I can do, at the moment."

"Hopefully it will all be over soon."

Ismat nodded. "For that I am hopeful."

Grover reached for his radio. "Jock, you lot all right out there?"

There was no answer.

"Jock?"

Still no answer.

"Jock?"

He reached for the Glock in his shoulder holster. Ismat was on edge instantly, looking around. "What is wrong?"

"I'm not sure." Grover climbed from his seat. "West."

A few moments later another agent emerged from the sitting room. "What's up?"

"I can't get through to the others. I'm going out to have a look."

Ross drew his own weapon. "All right, don't get too wet."

Grover grabbed an umbrella on the way out the door and stood on the stoop while he put it up. He went down the steps and splashed through a puddle on the sidewalk. "Shit."

Crossing the street to a BMW parked on the other side, he stepped onto the sidewalk, leaned down, and tapped on the passenger side window. When nothing happened, he frowned. "What the..."

He opened the door and a dead agent slumped sideways, hanging half out of the opening.

"Jesus Christ!" he exclaimed, grabbing for his Glock.

His hand had only just touched it when someone stepped up behind him and blew his brains out.

Then, using hand signals, the shooter directed his two comrades towards the house. They splashed across the street in the rain and disappeared inside. Not long after that came the sound of gunfire.

———

THE PERSISTENT SOUND of a phone ringing dragged Frank Fitzgerald from his slumber. With a few polite words he reached for it and was about to hit the answer button when his wife said, "Tell whoever it is to fuck off."

"I wish it was that simple, my dear," he replied. "Yes?"

It was Danny Travis. "Sir, we have a situation."

"I'm awake."

"Someone hit the Ismat safehouse tonight. They took out all of our agents and killed the Ismats as well."

"Bloody hell."

"I'm there at the moment."

"I'll be right over."

"Yes, sir."

The call ended and Fitzgerald swung his legs over the edge of the bed. Behind him his wife asked, "Can I expect you home anytime soon?"

"I'm not sure."

"Do be careful."

"Aren't I always?"

It took him thirty minutes to get dressed and drive through the rain-soaked London streets to the safehouse. He parked outside the police tape and walked the rest of the way after showing the officer on watch his identification.

Danny Travis, wet and cold, was waiting for him. "Sorry to get you out on a shit night like this, sir."

"Can't be helped, Danny. Walk me through it."

The MI5 agent led his boss over to the BMW. "Baker

and Chapman were killed in the car, sir. Both shot through the head. The blood spatter points to that."

He led Fitzgerald around the other side. Lying beside the vehicle was another body. "Lance Grover, sir. Shot in the head from behind. Executed."

"Shit."

"Whoever did this were professionals, sir."

"It would seem so, Danny."

"If you follow me, sir, I'll take you inside."

"Lead the way."

Inside the safehouse, they found Ross lying in the hallway. Travis said, "It looks like he heard them coming in, sir, and went to meet them. They shot him here. Jaalib Ismat is in the kitchen."

Ismat had been shot after standing up. His chair was turned over and the remains of his coffee spilled across the table onto the floor.

"His wife is upstairs in the bedroom, sir. They shot her while she was still in bed."

Fitzgerald nodded. "Has anyone notified the daughter yet?"

"No, sir."

"Have Lacey do it."

"Yes, sir."

A woman appeared, wet, her hair flattened by the rain. "Have Lacey do what? Oh, hello, sir. Bitch of a night to be out."

"Indeed, Miss Fox, indeed."

"What did you learn, Lace?" Travis asked.

"Apart from the fact it was a professional job? Not much. There is no brass and we can only assume that they parked their car further along the street."

Fitzgerald nodded. "Have the police door knock an extra block in every direction."

"Yes, sir."

"Do we have anything else?"

"Not at the moment."

"All right, this is what we're going to do. I want you to pull whoever you need out of bed and get them on this. I want security footage found and gone through from here to the Thames. Someone will have something, and I want it found."

"Yes, sir."

"And, Travis, find out where Simon Venables was tonight."

"Sir?"

"You heard me, get it done."

"Yes, sir."

Fitzgerald walked into another room and took out his cell. He dialed Anja Meyer and waited. "Hello?"

"Miss Meyer, Frank Fitzgerald. Sorry about the God-awful hour."

"What can I do for you, Frank?"

"Jaalib Ismat was murdered in our safehouse about ninety minutes ago. He and his wife."

"Damn it."

"Whoever did it took out four of my own men. I just need you to rule something in or out for me."

"Name it."

"Brian Warner."

"He is here in Amsterdam."

"I thought so. Thank you, Miss Meyer. Good night."

———

THE FOLLOWING MORNING, Travis and Lacey entered Fitzgerald's office with their reports. The outer office was abuzz with activity since the attack on the safehouse.

"Ladies first, Lacey," the MI5 commander said.

"Sir, I broke the news to the daughter and doubled the guard on her safehouse. The Royal Marine Commandos were considerate enough to give us a few of their chaps. So far, the questioning hasn't given us much, but we do have a vehicle. A black SUV with no plates."

"That will be our point of interest."

"Three men got out of it and then left in it, all within the time window of the murders. No facials on them at all."

"Keep after them," Fitzgerald said. "What about you, Danny?"

"That little matter you wanted me to look into came up empty. Venables was at his apartment all night."

"Can you check his phone records?"

"He's Six, sir, it'll be like trying to see through a fogged shower screen."

"Check his movements leading up to it."

"I did. The only place he went was The Stag and Horn."

"The gentlemen's club?"

Travis nodded. "That's right. The only people who go there are the rich and politicians."

Lacey said, "I'm betting he didn't go there to get his knob polished."

They both stared at her.

"What? We all know what goes on there. Dirty old men sitting around with topless waitresses who either serve them drinks or suck their dicks. Men only. It's a fucking archaic place that is just a brothel."

Travis shrugged. "She's right."

Fitzgerald nodded. "Find out why he was there. He had to be visiting someone. I want to know who. If we find that out, then maybe we might get some answers."

"Yes, sir."

"And if you go to the club, take Lacey with you. That'll shake the dirty old men up."

SHAKE THEM UP, it did.

"I'm sorry, sir, but the lady can't come in here," the man at the door said, looking Lacey up and down with his eyebrows raised.

"We work for the Security Service, mate, and we're both going inside. If you have a problem with that, get the manager."

Travis walked past him but when Lacey tried, the doorman stepped in front of her, placing an errant hand on her chest. Immediately, he looked down, realizing his mistake. He tried to remove it, but Lacey was too fast for him.

Her right hand came up and latched onto his index finger. With one swift movement, she snapped the finger like a twig, eliciting a high-pitched scream. The man dropped to his knees, clutching the hand to his stomach. "There are two people who can touch my tits, mate. One is my doctor, the other is the man I fuck. You are neither."

"Are you done, Lacey?" Travis asked with a roll of his eyes.

"I am now."

"Then, shall we go inside?"

"Fine."

Watching with disbelief the pair of agents entering through the revolving door, a man dressed in an immaculate suit almost had heart failure. He hurried out from behind the polished wood counter and shaking his hand, said, "No. No, no, no. She can't come in here. No women allowed."

They held up their identification. "We work for the Security Service."

"I don't care who you work for, young man, she can't come in here."

"Do you need me to suck your dick, guv'ner?" Lacey asked, exaggerating a Cockney accent.

The man gave her a horrified look. "I beg your pardon?"

"Well, you say no women allowed, but if I was one of the ones who sucked your dick I'd be more than welcome, right?"

"That—that is totally different. They aren't women. Not respectable ones, anyway."

"Good grief. Danny, can I shoot this geezer?"

"Not until we get some answers, Lace. Then I'll think about it."

Lacey looked at her watch. "Ten o'clock. I'm sure there are some early risers in the lounge."

Travis shook his head. "Your sense of humor is very droll."

They walked through the door and stopped. Lacey nodded. "So this is what a men's only club looks like."

A handful of chairs at tables were taken by men of various ages. A couple were on their own, the rest had company. Girls dressed in nothing but a thong in a variety of colors wandered about the room, serving or servicing.

"Give me strength," Lacey growled in a low voice.

Travis reached into his pocket for a picture of Venables. He approached one of the topless waitresses and asked, "Have you seen this man in here before?"

She shook her head and then noticed Lacey. "If you're here to work, love, then you should be out the back. If not, you don't belong here."

"I'm here to work, *love*, but not the way you think."

The waitress shrugged and walked off.

"What is the meaning of this?" a voice demanded.

The pair turned and saw a middle-aged man in a suit approaching them, an unhappy expression on his face.

Travis said, "Danny Travis and Lacey Fox. We're from the Security Service."

"I don't care where you are from, she does not belong here."

"Lacey goes where I go, mate. And as soon as we've finished our questions we shall leave. Failing that we shall classify this place as a terror organization and shut it down."

"You, you can't do that," the man blustered.

"Just watch me, mate." Danny stepped forward. He held up the picture of Venables and asked, "Has this man been in here recently?"

"I don't know," the man replied, not even bothering to look.

"It might help if you looked at the picture, sir," Lacey said.

"I don't need to."

Lacey looked around the room and saw a girl with her head bobbing up and down in a gentleman's lap. "Are you licensed, sir?"

"I beg your pardon?"

"Are you a licensed massage parlor?"

The man knew what she was getting at and looked at the picture. "He was in here yesterday."

"Do you know who he is?" Travis asked.

"I believe his name is Mister White?"

"Who was he here with?" Travis asked.

"I beg your pardon?"

"I know what he does for a living, and he doesn't earn enough to frequent an establishment like this. That means he was here visiting someone. Who?"

"I'm afraid—"

Lacey cleared her throat. "Are you going to answer the question or am I going to ruin that old gentleman's morning? Decide."

The man sighed. "He was here with Sir Michael Bennett. They meet here quite often."

"Thank you. Now, that wasn't so hard, was it?"

The two MI5 operatives turned and started to walk out of the lounge. Lacey said to Travis, "I think I'm going to take a shower for the next week, just to get the atmosphere of this place off me."

"Do you want to make the call or should I?" Travis asked.

"What call?" Lacey asked then a grin appeared, and then widened. "You are very nasty, Mister Travis."

"Well?"

"Oh, I'll make the call. Nothing would give me greater pleasure than to see that place shut down."

———

"HOW DID IT GO?" Fitzgerald asked them when they walked into his office.

Lacey said, "He was there seeing Sir Michael Bennett."

The MI5 boss nodded slowly. "That is interesting. Sir Michael has a wealth of money which would be more than enough to fund it."

"Fund what, sir?" Travis asked.

"Fund whatever it is they are up to."

"Why would he do that, sir?" Lacey asked.

"Three years ago, Sir Michael lost his wife and daughter to a terrorist attack here in London. It was around the time when we were having a resurgence in lone wolf warriors. Only it was a suicide bomb attack. Never stood a chance. If I had to guess, this is revenge for that."

"So, what Talon told you was true?" Travis asked.

"I never doubted that it was. Now we're starting to get proof."

"We still don't have any solid evidence that they were responsible for the attack on the safehouse," Lacey said.

"No. But Venables has more than enough assets to get the job done. SAS and private."

"Why would operators from the Regiment attack our own?"

"Just following orders, Lacey. Just following orders. Somewhere out there is a link. We just need to find it."

CHAPTER ELEVEN

Sofia, Bulgaria

HAWK SHRUGGED into his kit and loaded his MP5SD, ready to breach. Interpol agents were standing by on the sidelines after Hawk had insisted that he conduct the mission alone. He maintained that there was less chance of collateral damage that way.

"Be careful what you shoot at, Jake," Ilse said to him.

"I got this, Boss," he said to her keeping it professional. He put his comms in his ear and said, "Comms check, over."

Ilse nodded. "All good."

She tapped a few keys on her laptop and said, "ISR is up. You're good to go. Weapons free."

"Switch your bodycam on, Jake," a new voice said.

Hawk said, "Ah, I knew you wouldn't be far away, Alpha One."

"Someone has to oversee your antics," came the reply. "Are you sure about going in alone?"

"Can do it on my head."

"Let's hope you don't have to."

Hawk did a last check and climbed out of the van on

the sidewalk side. Across the street two men stood outside the door of a two-deck house. It was large, possibly an old boarding house. It looked as though it should have been condemned.

He leaned around the rear of the van and waited. Ilse said, "Alpha Two, ready."

"Bravo One, ready."

"Charlie One, ready."

Charlie One was the Interpol element.

"Kill the feed," Hawk said.

"Security feed down."

"Going hot." Hawk brought up the MP5 and targeted the first guard. He fired twice, dropping the man on the steps. Before his friend could move, Hawk switched his aim, and dropped the second. "Two X-rays down, moving in."

He hurried across the street. Climbing the stairs and stepping over the two dead guards, he opened the door.

As he went inside, Ilse said, "There is one X-ray inside to your right in the living area, Bravo One."

Hawk immediately turned right, found the threat, and fired. The guard grunted and slumped sideways on the sofa. "X-ray down."

The inside was totally different to the exterior. It had been well-maintained, which possibly meant the outside was for aesthetics only, to keep prying eyes away.

"There is a room to the left of the foyer, Bravo One, which looks to be clear. Proceed past the internal stairs and move to the dining area. There are two more X-rays there."

Hawk didn't bother answering. He walked past the staircase and through an opening which revealed two men sitting at a large table. The Brit hesitated. They were dressed in white uniforms. Some kind of medical staff. "What are you doing?" one of them blurted out.

"Be quiet or I'll kill you both. Stand up and turn around."

Both men did as they were ordered and Hawk zip-tied their hands. "If I have to come back here because you are making a noise, I will kill you. Understand?"

"Yes."

"Jake, there is an X-ray approaching you from the rear of the house. He's coming from the den. He's right on top of you."

The door across the room squeaked as it opened, and Hawk brought up the MP5 and fired. The armed man fell back through the opening, the only things visible his feet sticking out.

"X-ray down. Moving—wait one." Hawk turned to the men he'd just tied up. "Where are the girls?"

One of them shook his head, the other looked at the ceiling. "They are in the rooms upstairs."

"How many?"

"Six—no, five. One of them died."

Hawk almost shot him. "Where is Kalchev?"

"He is not here."

"Where?"

"He is making a delivery."

"What do you mean?" Hawk asked.

"Taking a couple of girls to a brothel."

"Shit. How many more guards are here?"

"No more."

"Alpha Two, tell me what you see," Hawk said into his comms.

"It looks clear, Jake. Just the heat signatures upstairs."

"Send in the cavalry."

———

"WE'RE MISSING AAMANI SINGH," Ilse said to Hawk.

The Interpol officers were processing everything and everyone. One walked past Hawk guiding a young woman drugged out of her mind. She staggered and Hawk caught her arm. "Easy, girl."

They kept walking. Hawk asked, "Are you sure she's not here?"

"Yes."

Hawk looked thoughtful. He returned to the dining room where the two men he'd tied up were being questioned by a female Interpol officer. "Do you mind if I interrupt for a moment?"

She shook her head. "No."

Hawk dug into his pocket for a cell. He bought up a picture and shoved it in the closest man's face. "Was she here?"

He nodded. "Yes."

"Where did she go?"

"Yerevan."

"Yerevan, Armenia?" Hawk asked.

"Yes."

"What for?" Hawk already knew the answer, but he wanted confirmation.

"Sold to a brothel."

"Jesus Christ," Hawk growled. "Now we have to deal with Armenian organized crime. Fuck."

"I'd better let the boss know we'll be a while," Ilse said.

"We're not leaving here before we get Kalchev," Hawk told her. He turned to the man he'd been talking to. "Now, tell me where that bastard is."

———

"WHAT ARE WE DOING, JAKE?" Ilse asked as they sat in the SUV across the street from the brothel's front door.

"What do you mean?" he replied. "We're waiting for Kalchev to appear."

"And you're just going to walk up to him and shoot him on the street?"

"Something like that."

"We're not assassins, Jake," Ilse reminded him.

"Sometimes the job calls for one, Ilse," he said to her. "This guy drugs girls, gets them addicted, and then uses them to make money. Sometimes they die. It's time it stopped. If you want to leave, go. I can do this on my own. I'll meet you at Whitey's place."

"No. I'll stay."

Hawk checked his handgun again. Then said, "Stuff it."

"What are you doing, Jake?"

"Going inside."

"Good grief."

Hawk climbed from the SUV and walked across the street. He approached the front door to the establishment and entered the foyer, moving across to the counter where a large breasted brunette woman wearing a red corset said, "Are you all right, sir?"

"Yeah, I'm looking for Kosta. I was told he was here."

"No, I'm sorry, he isn't here," the woman lied.

"I guess I'll check for myself."

The woman must have hit a silent alarm because a door on his left opened and a large man wearing black clothes and carrying a weapon appeared. Hawk drew his own gun and shot him in the chest. The man stopped in his tracks and fell to his knees. He looked like he was about to get back up, so Hawk shot him again.

The gunfire drew the rest of the guards. One appeared on the landing at the top of the stairs. Hawk pivoted and fired. The man fell forward, rolling down the stairs, leaving a bloody trail as he went.

A third man appeared in a doorway across the foyer. Hawk put two rounds into his chest and one in his head.

Then Hawk got shot. In the back.

The pain tore through him, but the Synoprathetic suit had done its job. He fought to turn and fire, a grimace etched on his face. "Fucking prick," he growled and shot his assailant four times.

Heading for another door, Hawk was forced back when he opened it, as bullets punched into the wood door jamb, sending splinters slicing through the air.

The Brit waited for a moment and then returned fire. The shots missed and he ducked back as more bullets came his way.

Hawk dropped to a knee and leaned back around the opening. He fired three shots before the slide locked back. One of his rounds put the shooter down, and while the Brit reloaded, the killer squirmed in a growing pool of his own blood.

Hawk stepped cautiously into the room; it was a living room and there were more people sheltering behind their chairs. However, there were no more shooters.

Across the room, Hawk saw the door with a sign on it. He knew enough to know that the man he wanted would be behind it.

As Hawk approached it, the door seemed to explode outwards. The Brit threw himself to the side as the bullets from within kept coming. He rolled away and came to his feet, approaching the door from the side.

He held his handgun in front of the door and shot through it four times.

More bullets punched through the thin veneer and thin, razor-sharp slivers sliced through the air.

"Christ," Hawk growled. He tried the door handle but found it locked. His attempt to open it brought forth a renewed and even deadlier fusillade.

Then it went silent. Reloading.

Hawk kicked the shit out of the door, and it flew back, smashing into the wall. Standing before him, near a desk were two men. One he assumed was Lassen Petkov, the man in charge of Kalchev's brothels. The other was Kalchev himself. The gun in Hawk's hand blasted to life.

Hawk fired four shots. Two for each man. By the time he was done, they were both dead.

———

Outside Amsterdam

Gray used the binoculars to scan the multitude of buildings before him. So far, he'd counted twenty people but undoubtedly there were more. Beside him, Slania observed with her own binoculars. "Twenty so far," she said.

"I concur," Gray agreed. "Probably more inside."

"What do you want to do?"

"Thin them out before we move in."

"It would be best."

"Copy, Boss?" Gray asked over the comms.

"Copy, Marcus." Anja was set up in an old delivery truck around a kilometer away from the abandoned mine.

"Boss, we have upwards of twenty X-rays onsite."

"Roger. It's your call."

"We're going to thin them down some before we move in. Standby."

"Copy. Standing by."

Gray settled in behind his DSR-Precision DSR-1 Sniper Rifle and looked for his first target. "Range?"

Beside him, Slania said, "Nine-hundred and thirty meters."

"Wind?"

"Negligible."

Gray made the adjustment and settled his eye in behind the scope. "Ready to fire."

"Send it."

The suppressed weapon slammed back into his shoulder. The projectile from the .308 Winchester Magnum round exploded from the barrel at just over 1,000 feet per second. It took roughly three seconds for the bullet to find a home. A lot can happen in that time. Thankfully it didn't.

The sentry dropped like a stone after the round punched through his chest. Gray changed his aim and picked out another target. "Range?"

"Same."

"Wind?"

"Same."

"Ready to fire."

"Send it."

The second sentry dropped.

For two more minutes, Gray and Slania worked together eliminating the outriders around the abandoned coal mine. When they were done, there were ten of them down. Slania said, "We'll need to do the rest the hard way."

"Roger that," Gray said. "Let's take a walk."

Because of the daylight the mission was that much harder, but they weren't about to let that stop them. Gray laid the sniper rifle to one side and picked up the suppressed H&K 416. His choice of weapon this time out other than the Bren2.

He and Slania slid down the gravel slope and sheltered behind an abandoned excavator. "We should be able to use the buildings for cover."

"Let's fuck up their day," Slania replied with a devious smile.

They were about to move when Anja said, "Bravo, hold."

Gray pressed his back against the excavator and asked, "What's up, Boss?"

"ISR has picked up an underground tunnel system beneath the area where you are. Could be someone has converted the underground mine to some kind of fortress."

"Someone's been busy."

"You'll need to find a way in if you want to get Warner. My guess is that's where he is."

"Copy."

Gray came out from behind the excavator and moved towards the first building. It was small, not much more than a tool shed. He leaned around the side and saw a pair of sentries chatting together. Using hand signals, Gray indicated that he wanted Slania to take the one on the left while he took care of the other one.

Then, while facing away from her, he used his fingers and counted down until he reached zero.

Slania tapped him on the shoulder, and he moved. They both came clear of the shed's exterior, Gray taking a wider path. They opened fire at the same time, only stopping when the X-rays were both down.

"Good kill," Gray said to his partner.

They continued to push forward until they reached a larger shed. Finding an open door, they went inside. The plan was to use it to move further in.

"Alpha One, this is Bravo."

"Good copy, Bravo."

"Shed two is clear. Looks like whatever was in here was cleaned out years ago."

"Roger. I think you'll find the entry to the underground system in a large shed to the north. There seems to be extra guards around it."

"Copy. Moving to that location."

Gray opened the far door and looked around. The path to the next building was clear. They broke cover,

Gray covering right and front while Slania covered left and rear.

"Contact—" Slania started before she let her voice trail away as she opened fire. The X-ray who had appeared dropped face down onto the gravel covered ground.

She kept her 416 trained on the area where she'd just killed the man, expecting another to appear. "We need to get below ground before they sound the alarm, Marcus," she said.

"Tell me about it."

Finally, they reached the building in question. And the sentries that went along with it. Four of them.

Gray said, "You take the two on the right, I'll take those on the left."

"It sounds good to me."

"Let's do it then."

They came out from cover and while walking forward, opened fire. Two of the guards fell to the ground while the two remaining ones brought their weapons up to defend themselves. However, Gray and Slania fired again with their 416s and the guards soon joined their comrades.

They kept moving forward and Gray opened the large sliding door which led into the shed. They had only just stepped foot into it when Anja's voice came over the comms. "Bravo, hold position."

"What's up, Boss?"

"We have a helicopter inbound from the west."

"One of theirs?" Slania asked.

"I'm not sure."

They waited for a minute before Gray said, "I need a go or no go, Boss."

"Hold position."

After another few moments they could hear the helicopter. "Bravo, it looks to be a Chinook. Get out of there, now."

Slania glanced at Gray. "What's going on?"

"Chinook means Brits. The boss will be betting they are SAS. Which means Venables has sent a team to clean up."

"Oh, shit. Friends are now enemies."

"That's it. Let's move."

They circled around the landing zone and paused to watch the helicopter land. The ramp came the rest of the way down and twenty SAS troopers deployed, moving straight for the shed where the tunnel entrance supposedly was. Gray said, "Come on, it's time we weren't here. Coming to you, Boss."

CHAPTER TWELVE

Yerevan, Armenia

BY DAY, the city of Yerevan belonged to the people, by night, it belonged to whoever could control it. At that moment, it was one man. Garin Kasabian, or The Butcher.

Kasabian was the boss of everything organized crime within the city limits. Prostitution, drugs, bribery, fraud, arms dealing, murder—anything that could turn a dollar. He had been one of Medusa's bigger customers, turning over a staggering five-hundred prostitutes every year.

Outside of the city, there was a plot of land of almost five acres. It was one of the best fertilized plots in Armenia. Those in the know called it The Prostitutes Graveyard.

"Are we sure someone is coming tonight?" Hawk asked Ilse as they sat waiting in their SUV positioned in a stand of trees.

"My source says yes."

"Christ, hopefully this isn't a dead end."

"Bad pun, Jake." Ilse shook her head.

"Shit, sorry, unintentional."

They had arrived in Armenia that afternoon. Ilse had met with her informant, and now they were staking out the plot called The Prostitutes Graveyard for a man they hoped would know about the girl they sought: Aamani Singh.

"Heads up, we've got a vehicle approaching."

Hawk looked out through the window and saw a pair of headlights bouncing over the ground. He reached for his MP5SD and waited.

The vehicle stopped and the headlights went out. Hawk grabbed his NVGs and placed them over his head. "They're getting out. Two of them."

Ilse put her own on. The two men went to the rear of the small truck and opened the door. "Looks like they're getting the bodies out."

Hawk said, "Let's move."

Climbing from the SUV, they used the dark to their advantage. When they were within weapon range, Hawk raised his MP5 and lined the laser sight up on the closest man. He squeezed the trigger and the man dropped. Beside him, Ilse shot the second guy in the leg. He cried out in pain and fell beside his friend.

Hurrying forward, Hawk called out, "Down! Stay the fuck down."

The wounded man wasn't going anywhere as he clutched his wounded leg. Hawk shone a flashlight on him and said to Ilse, "I hope you speak Armenian."

She squatted beside the wounded man and slapped him across the face. "Hey, look at me."

The man looked up, his face was a mask of pain. Ilse said, "Don't worry about your leg. Worry about me. Answer my questions."

"But I am wounded."

"I don't give a shit. You will answer my questions, or my friend here will shoot you."

"Okay, okay."

Ilse took out a picture of Aamani Singh. "Tell me about this girl."

"I do not know her."

"You haven't looked yet."

The man stared at her. "And I still do not know her. It is more than what my life is worth. Garin will kill me."

Hawk leaned over him. "Listen, mate, you obviously don't know how much fucking trouble you are in. It's time to man up or I'm going to put a fucking bullet between your eyes. You won't need to worry about Garin."

The man looked at Ilse, confused. "What? What did he say?"

"He said, 'You're a dead man.'"

"No, no, no, no. I will tell you whatever you want to know."

"Look at the picture."

The man looked. "I think I have seen her. But she could be moved by now."

"Then tell me. Who knows?"

"Lilit will know."

"Where will I find Lilit?" Ilse asked.

"At home with Maraal," the man said.

"Who is Maraal?" Ilse asked.

"Detective Maraal Hakobyan, her husband."

Ilse looked at Hawk. "This just doesn't get any better."

"Why?"

"Because the one who knows where the girl is, is married to a cop."

"Shit."

———

"THIS IS WHERE THEY LIVE?" Ilse asked the man sitting beside her in the rear of the SUV. They were parked outside a tidy two story home with two steps.

"Yes."

"Get out," she ordered.

"What?"

"Get out and go away. If I ever see you again, I will kill you."

The man couldn't believe his luck. He opened the door and began to limp away. Hawk turned and looked in the back. "I wonder if we can knock on the door?"

Ilse took out her Glock. "Let's find out."

They screwed on their suppressors and climbed out of the SUV, crossing the street, and walking up the steps. As he went, Hawk shot out the streetlamp.

"I've got a camera here, Jake."

"Kill it."

Ilse shot it and then rang the doorbell. A few moments later, a voice said from the other side, "Who is it?"

It was a man's voice, most likely Lilit's husband, Maraal. Ilse said, "I'm sorry to disturb you, but there is trouble in the house next door. I was told you were a police officer, so I came to you for help."

There was a long pause before the man said, "All right. I'll just open the door."

As soon as he heard the locks disengage, Hawk kicked the door, smashing it into the knees of the person on the other side. He followed up and saw the man on the floor, a gun in his hand. Hawk's foot came down upon it and heard the bones in the man's wrist break.

Maraal cried out as pain shot through his arm. Hawk brought a knee down on the policeman's chest, pinning him. "Where is Lilit?"

"Fuck you."

"Lilit?" Hawk asked again, increasing the pressure.

There was a sound from upstairs and the Brit looked at Ilse. She nodded, raised her Glock, and started up to the second floor. Behind her, Hawk hit Maraal twice, knocking him out, and then followed Ilse up the staircase.

144

They reached the landing and were about to move to a room at the end of the hallway when the door flew open, and gunfire erupted.

A woman, standing in only panties and tank top, filled the void, holding a handgun in each fist. Hawk and Ilse ducked back to either side of the door and Hawk growled, "A frigging holiday about now would be good."

"Hold your fire," Ilse called out. "We just want to talk."

"You want to die, bitch," came the reply.

"Let me shoot her," Hawk said.

"No, we need her alive."

"I won't kill her, promise."

"Like your track record is great."

"I've made mistakes."

"Lilit, we just want to talk."

More gunfire hammered out along the short hallway. "Just so you know, I have friends on the way."

"Shit," Hawk said. "Fine, you shoot her."

"Jake, what are you doing?"

"Just shoot her."

He stepped out into the hallway, exposing himself. Lilit fired and the bullet punched into his chest, bringing him to his knees. Stunned by his stupidity, Ilse was slow to react, allowing the woman to shoot him in the chest again.

"For crying out loud," Hawk moaned as he started to fall. "Shoot the bitch."

Ilse came out into the hallway and fired. The bullet from her Glock kicked the left leg out from under Lilit

With a cry of pain, she hit the floor, her handguns spilling from her grasp. Ilse hurried forward and kicked them out of reach and then secured the woman while she was down.

Behind Ilse, Hawk staggered to his feet. "Better late than never, I guess."

"You're an idiot," she snarled at him, dragging Lilit to her feet. "We need to get her out of here before the others show up."

Hawk grabbed the woman by her arm and said to Ilse, "Lead the way."

As she walked past him, she said, "You're still an idiot."

———

THEY STOPPED at a secure underpass just off one of the main freeways which was still under development. The wound in Lilit's leg had been bandaged and the bleeding stopped. Ilse stood in front of her and shone a light on the picture she held up. "This girl. Where is she?"

"I know nothing," she said bitterly.

"We were told differently. All we want to know is where she is, and we'll—"

WHAP! WHAP!

Two bullets punched into Lilit's chest, killing her instantly. "Bloody hell," Hawk exploded, ducking down and taking cover, dragging Ilse with him.

Out of the darkness four men appeared, moving with military precision. They opened fire, pinning the two of them in place.

"We can't stay here," Hawk said.

"I agree, but where the hell do we go? Look around, Jake, there is nothing."

"If in doubt, run," Hawk said sounding jovial.

"Great."

"You ready? We empty a mag each at these pricks and then we go."

Ilse shrugged. "I guess it's all we have."

They both opened fire at the advancing figures with their Glocks, pumping shot after shot at them until the slides locked back. "Go!" Hawk shouted.

Then they ran. Just as fast as they could.

Both of them took shelter behind a concrete pillar. Bullets began taking chips, sending shards of concrete whizzing off into the night, leaving pock marks in the previously smooth surface.

"Where to now?" Ilse asked.

Hawk fired at the approaching gunmen and saw one go down, wounded in the leg. He glanced around but the dark made it hard. "Move to the next pillar."

They leapfrogged back, using the pillars as cover until, reaching the end of the construction, they ran out of them. Ilse fired the rest of a second magazine and reloaded. "I've got one mag left, Jake."

Hawk glanced back over his shoulder at the construction site. "In there."

Once more they broke cover and ran. This time there was a little more cover than before with equipment and machinery. As they ducked behind a crane, bullets ricocheted off its metal frame, a window in the cabin blowing out.

Overhead there were large floodlights used by the construction crews when they worked nights. Hawk looked around and saw it on a pole. A fuse box which he assumed would light the floodlamps. "Wait here."

Circling safely around to the pole, Hawk found the box locked. He made short work of it with a quick shot and opened it. Finding what he was looking for, he flicked the switch.

The effect was instant. The lights illuminated the whole construction area, including the three remaining killers who were fighting hard to get to Hawk and Ilse.

Blinded momentarily by the sudden brightness, the shooters paused. Ilse came out into the open and fired at the first of the three shooters. Two in the chest, one in the head. From near the fuse box, Hawk fired his own weapon, putting the next shooter down.

Still dazzled by the bright lights, the final killer never stood a chance. They both fired at him, killing him within a heartbeat.

Hawk rushed forward to check for identification. They were clean, but when he checked for tattoos, he hit the jackpot. "Fucking Russian prison fodder."

"What do you mean?" Ilse asked.

"Tattoos. They're here after the bounty."

"We need to find Bondarev and put him in the ground," Ilse growled.

"I know, but we have more pressing matters to deal with," Hawk reminded her.

They walked back to the SUV and checked Lilit. She was already getting cold. "What do we do now?" Hawk asked out loud.

"We go to the source," Ilse said.

"What? Kasabian?"

"Yes."

"How do we do that?"

"We watch and wait."

"Crap on a goat."

_____

London, England

"Warner has been taken care of," Venables said. "I had a team take him out at one of his bases. The problem was, someone else had been there before us and I think they saw them start their operation."

"Your friends at Talon?"

"I believe so."

"That will have to wait. We have another problem. There were some MI5 people at the club asking about you. And me. This will be fallout from where Jaalib Ismat and his wife were killed."

148

"What do you want me to do?"

"Put a team on them."

"Do you have any names?"

"Danny Travis and Lacey Fox."

"I'll do it when I leave here."

"Is there any news on that other matter?" Bennett asked.

"I'm waiting on word. It looks like Farhadi might be in Brussels."

"What would he be doing in Brussels?"

"Sending us a 'fuck you'"

———

Amsterdam

"He's in Brussels," Slania said.

"Farhadi?" Anja asked.

"Yes."

"Tell me why?"

"That's where his money is. I did some digging, and he has an account with the Brussels Global Banking Executive Branch."

"How much?" asked Ilse.

"Two billion."

"Are you reading that right?"

"Yes. Do you want me to freeze his account?"

"No. I want him being as normal as possible. Recall Ilse and Jake. I want everyone in Brussels within twenty-four hours."

"What about Aamani Singh?"

"Put Interpol onto it. Tell Ilse to give them everything they have. From now on, we go after Farhadi."

———

"You have got to be kidding," Hawk snapped. "They're pulling us off this thing to go to Brussels?"

"We hand it over to Interpol, Jake. It's not like we're just dumping it."

"The hell it isn't."

"Listen, it's all getting too messy. We're spread out and combat ineffective."

"Speak for yourself."

"We stop Farhadi, then we stop Venables. After that we go after Bondarev."

"I don't like it."

"It's the way it has to be," Ilse said.

"What's he doing in Brussels anyway?"

"That's where his money is," Slania said over the video link.

Hawk shook his head. "No. There has to be something else. Another reason for him to be there."

"Whoa," Slania said. "Someone just took a big chunk of money out of his account."

"How much?" Hawk asked.

"Fifty million."

"It's a payment for something," Hawk said. "Find out where it went."

Slania worked her keyboard, her fingers tapping in the background. "It looks like the payment went to an account in the Caymans."

"Find out whose it is."

"It belongs to a company called Tarrant Holdings. It looks to be a shell company owned by—Unilateral Possessions. It's based in Russia."

"I have a bad feeling about this," Hawk said.

"So you should. The owner of Unilateral Possessions is Nikita Bondarev."

"It would be," Hawk muttered.

"Slania, do you have any idea what Farhadi just bought off Bondarev for fifty-million?"

"Not yet, but whatever it is, it can't be good."

CHAPTER THIRTEEN

Brussels, Belgium

"INTERPOL FOUND AAMANI SINGH," Slania told Hawk when they met face to face after their flight arrived in Brussels. "They've got her under guard in a hospital before they fly her out."

"That's something, I guess," Hawk said. "Is there any update on Farhadi?"

"No, he's been quiet."

"Nothing on what the money was for?"

"No."

"There has to be something," said Anja. "Give me a moment and I'll make a call."

She walked away from her team and took out her cell, dialing a familiar number, and waited.

"Anja, my dear, this is becoming a habit," Graf noted.

"I need your help, Harald."

"Anything, just name it."

"How up to date are your intel briefs?"

"We get them every hour," Graf said.

"I need to know why our POI paid Nikita Bondarev fifty-million."

"Interesting," Graf said. "Do you know what Bondarev actually does, Anja?"

"He's involved with oil. He has his own private army."

"He also oversees the Gulag system."

"But the Gulags were abolished sixty years ago," Anja pointed out.

"They were supposed to be, but in certain parts the forced labor camps are still there," Graf explained. "One of those Gulags holds terrorists. Women and men. We received intelligence yesterday that a train left that camp with one-hundred women on it."

"Where is it bound?" Anja asked.

"Pakistan."

"We need to stop it," Anja said.

"Why would you do that?" Graf asked.

"Because I bet that every one of those women he just bought are Black Widows. It will be a mixing pot of race, but you can be certain of one thing—those women on that train are being prepped for something. Something big."

"Then we need to stop it permanently," Graf said.

"No. Some of them can be rehabilitated. Some will have been forced into it. Those are the ones we need to rescue."

"Good luck with that," Graf said.

"I need your help, Harald," Anja said.

"And how am I supposed to help you?"

"I need the KSK."

The call disconnected and Anja turned back to her team. "I know that look," Ilse said. "We have a mission."

"Yeah," agreed Hawk. "And usually it takes some death-defying feat to pull it off."

Anja gave a grim smile. "Ladies and gentlemen, we need to stop a train."

"I knew it," Hawk said. "I bloody knew it."

"The money, according to German Intelligence, was to buy prisoners from a Russian Gulag."

Hawk scoffed. "Gulag? Really?"

"In spite of what we think we know, apparently the Russians still find it hard to let some things go. Now, on that train are believed to be Black Widows."

"Crap," Gray growled. "If they get back into the system, then everything is screwed."

"I agree. Slania, find out all you can on who might be on that train. Farhadi is up to something, and I want to know—" Anja frowned. "What is it?"

Slania had been looking at something on her computer screen. "A team of mercenaries just hit a Brussels hotel. Looking at this report. It's a shit show."

"Who was at that hotel, Slania?"

The tech looked up. "Akmal Farhadi."

"Can we get footage?" Anja asked.

A minute later the large screen in their mobile ops room lit up with feed from inside the hotel. The first thing they saw was a team of five shooters moving through the hotel lobby. A security guard had had his back to them and when he turned, they shot him where he stood.

"Christ," grated Hawk. "They're SAS."

"How do you know?" Anja asked.

"The way they move."

"He's right," Gray said, agreeing. "You serve with a group long enough, you get to know them inside and out."

"That's all I can get," Slania said.

"It's enough," Hawk replied. "That will be Venables."

Anja sighed. "Fine, back to the train. I want to know everything about it and what its destination is. We are wheels up in thirty minutes."

"But where are we going?" Ilse asked.

"I have no idea."

———

"Everyone, gather around," Anja said as the plane hit a pocket of turbulence. "This is what we have so far. The train is on its way to Pakistan. There it will terminate, and the women will disembark. This is the troubling part. Only around forty percent are believed to be Black Widows. The rest are Russian political prisoners. Lawyers, opposition politicians, protestors, anyone young enough to make a good wife for Jihadi fighters."

Ilse looked at Anja. "He's preparing an army."

"Quite possibly. The question is where? However, the ultimate goal of this operation is to stop that train and rescue the sixty percent."

"What about the other forty percent?" Hawk asked.

"They will most likely try to kill you. Expect a good proportion to be armed. Jake, Marcus, find me a way onto that train. I want it stopped. You have until we land to come up with a plan. You will have a team of KSK Commandos to work with. Let me know when you are ready."

"We'll need a picture of the train," Hawk said.

"Slania?"

The wireless printer beside her whirred. She picked up the picture and passed it to Hawk. "If you need anything else, just call out."

Hawk and Gray sat down and started to work out the particulars. Gray said, "Both ends at the same time?"

Hawk nodded. "Yeah, that would be best. Two teams of four. Any more than that will create too much congestion."

"Secure the loco. Two men."

"I agree." Hawk thought for a moment. "There are three carriages. The political prisoners will be in the center one. The others will be filled with the Widows. Just speaks for itself."

155

Gray said, "How about this. We take extra shooters and they secure the carriages at each end. The only one we breach is the one with the political prisoners."

"Then what do we do with the other two? We can't just plant explosives and kill them. The boss won't let us do that just in case."

"Then they have to be cleared. All three at the same time from both ends. Using tear gas."

"Sixteen shooters max with a reserve," Hawk said.

"I think so."

"Four helicopters that put us on top of the train."

"Yes."

"God, I love this job."

"I'm glad someone does."

———

Tajikistan

The German KSK Commandos were flown in before Talon had even arrived. Led by a bear of a man named Hans Schmidt, they were in a hangar at a secluded airfield going over the plan of attack for the mission.

Hawk said, "I'll have overall command of the mission. Hans will be my second in command. Are you good with that, Hans?"

"Of course."

"Okay. This is how things will go down. The helos will come in from the rear of the train and drop each team on the rear carriage. I will lead team one. Once we're down, we push forward ready to secure the front carriage. Marcus will take the second, Hans the third. The fourth helo will have the two-man team to secure the loco. They will rope down and secure that once we start securing the carriages. We go in with tear gas and flashbangs. Consider everyone in one and three to be hostile. Take no chances with two. They may all be political prisoners, but be situational aware. Any questions?"

They all remained silent. The questions that had to be asked were asked earlier. Hawk nodded. "All right, we go in an hour once it is dark. Good luck."

———

THEY WERE all dressed in black, had NVGs pulled down, and looked like aliens from another universe. Each man was armed with MP5SDs and carried gas masks. Hawk was in the lead MH-6 Little Bird Helicopter as it flew low and hard, following the rail line. The landscape was green through his NVGs as it scooted by below. In the helicopter with him were three KSK men, and although he'd never operated with these men, he had every confidence that they would prove their mettle.

"One minute to target," the pilot's voice filled Hawk's comms.

"Roger, one minute."

He looked at the others in his squad. They gave him the thumbs up. The Brit leaned out a little further and looked forward. As the helicopter skidded around a bend in the track, he saw the train ahead of them.

"Thirty seconds."

Hawk turned his head and looked back behind them. Each helicopter was still there, turning and weaving like a flying snake. The Brit checked his gear once more and by the time he was finished, the helicopter was hovering over the last carriage. Moments later, Hawk stepped onto the rooftop of the last carriage, followed by the rest of the first team. They remained crouched while the helicopter lifted away, then they moved forward, taking themselves out of the way of the next lift.

Soon all three teams were down and on the rooftop of the train carriages. Hawk led his team to the first carriage, jumping across the gaps in between like stunt doubles in an action movie. Upon reaching their target carriage, he used hand signals to prep his first pair.

Soon all teams were ready to breach.

"Masks on," Hawk said. Then, "Cut the lights."

Things went dark. "Gas out."

Each team opened the doors at their respective ends of the carriages and threw the tear gas cannisters in. Once deployed, Hawk counted down saying, "Three...two... one...go, go, go."

Then it was time for the teams to utilize their stun grenades. The explosions from within signaled two things. Screams from the women, and the go for the teams.

Hawk went first and saw the carnage that the gas and stun grenades had caused. Just inside the door was a guard with an AK-47. She was doubled over, coughing. Hawk hit her behind the ear, and she dropped like a stone. At the other end of the carriage came the sound of gunfire which stopped abruptly.

Hawk scouted. "Sit down! Everyone sit the fuck down!"

Another woman appeared with an AK. She pointed it at Hawk. "Ah, fuck," he growled and shot her in the chest.

Her finger pressed the trigger and as she went down, the weapon sprayed the carriage with a deadly, scything fire. The rounds found flesh and three more women died.

"Bloody hell," Hawk snarled.

He pressed forward, checking the women as he went. He caught the eye of one who was fidgeting in her seat. He stared at her, and she panicked. She reared up and tried to shoot him with an AK-74.

The commando with Hawk fired before she could and her head snapped back as the bullet punched into it.

As he kept moving, Hawk heard the fourth team say into his comms, "Delta Four is down, the train is under our control."

Suddenly Hawk lurched as the train began to slow. At the other end of his carriage, Hawk saw the other team members as they came towards him. Then they disappeared in a ball of flame as a grenade from a Widow detonated in front of them.

———

BEFORE ENTERING THE THIRD CARRIAGE, Hans Schmidt let the MP5SD hang by its strap and he drew his HK USP Tactical 9mm. He paused for a moment and waited for Hawk's order to go. Once it came, he threw in the flashbang, waited, and then moved.

There was an armed guard just inside the door. Like in the first carriage it was a woman. She was doubled over, coughing.

The USP came down and she dropped to the floor.

"Down, everyone, get down!" Hans shouted.

Another woman started spraying bullets from an AK-74 towards the voice. Her bullets found multiple targets, all of them her own kind. Hans set his jaw firm, ignoring the danger, unhappy about having to kill a woman. But he shot her anyway.

The two groups finished securing the carriage and Hans was about to give another order when he heard the blast in the forward carriage.

Hans looked at his men. "Wait here, keep everything secure. He turned and hurried out of the carriage and into carriage number two. Gray had already secured it and was moving towards the first carriage. Hans forced his way through and caught up with the former para. "What was that?"

"I have an idea."

The glass in the carriage door was gone, blown outward by the detonation from within. Through the jagged opening Gray could see the bloody carnage inside the carriage. He dragged the door open, and a maimed woman fell into his arms, a bloody stump where her arm used to be, and half of her face burned off. The former para tried not to recoil at the ghastly sight, but she wasn't the only one—there were others, many others, including two commandos.

Gray looked up and saw Hawk at the other end of the carriage. "Are you okay?"

"I'll live."

"What the fuck happened?"

"Some silly cow let go a grenade. We need medivac."

"Yeah, and then some."

Hawk shook his head and tried to block out the screams. "What a bloody cockup."

Tajikistan

"What intel did we recover?" Anja asked.

"All we know is that they were headed for northern Pakistan," Slania said. "Somewhere in the mountains."

"What is in those mountains?" Anja asked.

"We think a training camp," Ilse replied. "For terrorists."

"Are they Farhadi's terrorists?" Anja asked.

"Yes, well at least we assume so."

"So, he was topping up his force with the Black Widows and the others were going to be war brides, is that it?"

"Most probably."

"Well, what do we do now? I'm open to all suggestions."

"We start tying off all the frayed ends," Hawk said. "Venables, Farhadi, and Bondarev."

"Add a fourth name to the list," Anja said. "Michael Bennett, Member of Parliament."

"What's he got to do with it?" Gray asked.

"He's the one responsible for the operation which we find ourselves mixed up in."

"This is a job for Marcus and me," Hawk said. "It all ends in no good way, Boss. It's going to be a black operation. No one lives."

"I know, Jake. German intelligence, remember?"

"You don't want to be part of this, ma'am. Not when we go after a Brit MP."

"If you go after a British MP, it'll be on my orders," Anja informed him.

"Yes, Boss."

"Ilse, find Venables. We'll go after him first. With him out of the way we can go after Farhadi without having to worry about him popping up and shooting us in the back."

"Yes, boss."

"I have a call to make."

The others went about their business while Anja called Frank Fitzgerald. When he answered he said, "Good work with the train, Miss Meyer. Brilliant, actually."

"We were lucky," she replied. "We're going after Venables. He needs to be stopped."

"How hard?"

"If we do it right, he won't walk away. We need him gone."

"I understand."

"Then there is the Bennett issue."

"You can't go around killing British MPs, Miss Meyer," Fitzgerald pointed out.

"I'm not going to kill him, Frank."

"I don't like the way you said that. I don't want to see any of your people near Bennett."

"Then don't look."

"Bloody hell. Why are you telling me this?"

"Call it a courtesy."

"I'll call it stupidity. If you don't get it right, then you'll be wanted all over the globe. The government won't care that he was mixed up in whatever shit it was. They'll just see you and your people committing murder."

"They won't even know it was us."

———

"I FOUND VENABLES," Ilse said. "He's in Pakistan."

"What's he doing there?" Anja asked.

"Tracking Azhaan Imam. He's got an SAS team with him."

"Who is Azhaan?" Anja asked.

"He is on the British Terror Watch List. He was supposedly behind the bombing of the British Embassy in Islamabad three years ago. However, there was no proof."

"So what is the link with him and the others?"

"All of the men who have died so far, know Farhadi but they've never met each other."

"His network?" Anja asked.

"Yes, it would seem so."

Anja looked at Ilse thoughtfully. "There has to be a link between Bennett and Farhadi. Find it. The man is dismantling his network for a reason."

"Yes, ma'am."

Hawk opened the door just as Ilse was walking out. She looked at him and said, "You. Come. Help."

He looked at Anja and shrugged before turning to follow Ilse.

"What are we doing?" Hawk asked her after they had entered the mobile ops room. Ilse looked around and then kissed him. He raised his eyebrows. "Whatever it is, I'm in."

"Shut up and kiss me back."

Once they were done, he asked, "Now what?"

"We need to find the link between Farhadi and Bennett," Ilse said. "From what we've been able to put together, Venables and Bennett are dismantling his network."

"Which is why Farhadi sent shooters after Venables."

"Quite possibly."

Hawk sat down and thought for a moment. Then he said, "It's personal."

Ilse nodded. "It points to that, but how?"

"What makes things like this personal?" Jake asked, steepling his fingers below his chin deep in thought.

"An attack on oneself or the family."

"Bennett lost his family in a suicide bomb attack."

Ilse sat down in front of a computer and brought up an old newspaper clipping. The picture she found was of a woman in her late fifties and another around twenty-three. "Wife and daughter."

Another picture came up. This time the bodies were torn to shreds. Ghastly, gruesome. Hawk stared at the picture. "Wait, go back."

Ilse switched back to the other picture. "Look at her forearm."

"The tattoo?"

"Yes."

"Now go back to the other picture," Hawk told her.

She did as he said. For a moment she couldn't grasp what Hawk was alluding to, then she saw it. "The tattoos are different."

"Yes, they are."

"She isn't his daughter."

"That would be my guess."

"Do you think he knows?"

"I'd bet my left nut he does."

"Don't do that," Ilse said. "You might lose, and I still have a use for it."

He grinned at her. "You're a wicked girl."

A minute later they were standing in front of Anja explaining their theory. Ilse said, "There is only one way to find out."

Anja nodded. "I'll get it done."

Moments later, she was talking to Frank Fitzgerald again.

"That is a good catch if it's true," Fitzgerald said. "I'm not sure how it got past intelligence. Especially about the daughter. Are you sure that it's not her?"

"My people are."

"Then I'd better put my people on it."

CHAPTER FOURTEEN

London, England

"OH, IT'S YOU AGAIN," the man behind the counter at the club said.

"Good afternoon to you, too," Lacey said to him with a sarcastic smile.

"What do you want this time?"

"Michael Bennett," Travis replied.

The man shook his head. "No. Absolutely not. Do you know who he is?"

"It's our job to know who he is," Lacey replied. "Now, if we go in there, are we going to find him decent or getting his knob polished?"

"You'll find none of that goes on here," the man shot back at her.

"We'll see, shall we?"

Travis and Lacey stopped on the far side of the doorway. Things were very different this time. They looked at each other and smiled. All the scantily-clad waitresses had been replaced by waiters who were fully clothed. "I guess that call worked."

"I see our man at two o'clock," Travis said.

"Let's go and yank his chain."

Bennett looked up at them and asked, "What does the Security Service want?"

"We would like to talk to you," Travis said.

Bennett looked at Lacey. "Make an appointment. Now get out, there are no women allowed."

Lacey gave him her best smile. "Sir, my name is Lacey Fox. We're here to talk but if you refuse, we will take you back and pull out your fucking fingernails until you do."

"So uncouth."

"Such a fuckwit."

Bennett's face hardened. "I could have your job with a click of my fingers, you bitch."

"Start fucking clicking, asshole."

"All right, enough," Travis said. "Mister Bennett, we came here to ask questions, but if you keep this up, we will take you back."

The MP took a sip from his glass of whiskey and placed it back on the low table. "I'll give you two minutes. No more."

"Then we'd best not fuck around," Lacey said. "Did you know that your daughter wasn't killed with your wife?"

He stared at them.

"Wow, that was quick," Lacey said. "You see, Mister Bennett, we're trained to know when people are lying. Sometimes it takes a while. You just shit and broke the record."

"I beg your pardon?"

"We have proof that the young woman who died beside your wife wasn't her. Your lying just a minute ago, also proves that she didn't. It also proves that you knew."

Travis sat down opposite Bennett and said, "Shall we start again?"

"There is nothing to discuss."

"You know what I think," Travis said. "I think you

166

know your daughter isn't dead. I think she is with Farhadi, which is why you're trying to burn his kingdom to the ground. Everyone that you and Venables have gone after is known to Farhadi. But you screwed up when you went after the man himself and *his* daughter died. Then he came after Venables once he worked out what was happening. To do that he used Talon."

Bennett didn't speak.

Lacey cleared her throat and said, "When we worked out that it wasn't your daughter we looked into her history. She worked for Farhadi's company. Was she fucking him?"

Bennett lurched to his feet threateningly. "Watch your mouth," he hissed.

"We don't know how she did it, but she did. We'll work that out later. But when you found out, it must have sent you off the deep end."

He glared at her.

"Did you deliberately have his daughter killed? Revenge?"

"No, it was an accident. We needed her to get to him like the others."

"But after you used her, it didn't matter, did it?"

"I didn't give a tinker's toss about them."

"Where is your daughter?" Travis asked.

"I don't know."

"You don't know, or you aren't telling?"

"I do not know. All that I can tell you is that she is still alive and in the hands of that bastard."

"Why would she be with him?"

Bennett hesitated. "Because you were right. She was sleeping with him."

"Who was with your wife?" Travis asked.

"It is thought that it was the bomber. A Black Widow. My wife was on her own that day. I had the authorities break the news that my daughter had died alongside my wife. I couldn't face the fact that she had gone to that bastard."

"So you said she was dead."

"She *was* dead."

"Do you know it was the truth?"

"What?"

"That she went with him, willingly. Maybe he just took her."

He ignored the question.

Travis stood up. "We'll need to talk to you again."

They walked outside and Travis turned to Lacey. "What do you think?"

"I think he's lying about something."

"Then someone needs to find out the truth before this war grows even bigger."

Tajikistan

"Everyone, listen up," Anja said to her people. "I have news. MI5 had a talk to Michael Bennett. Apparently, his daughter, according to him, is still alive and we think in Pakistan. Word is that she was sleeping with Farhadi. The young lady who died with Bennett's wife was actually the bomber. Things were altered to make it look like it did. What we have to do is find out if it's true. To do that, we need to locate Lisa Bennett and get her out."

"There might be someone who knows where she is," Hawk said. "Azhaan Imam."

"My thoughts exactly. So, we're going to Pakistan, and we're going to kidnap and question, Azhaan."

"Before Venables can do anything to him?" Ilse asked.

"Right out from under his nose."

"If he interferes?" Gray asked.

"Then we put him down hard before he can do the

same to us. It's time to stop playing around and do a proper job."

Hawk sighed. "I miss Santorini."

Anja turned her gaze to Ilse. "By the time we land, I want you and Slania to have Azhaan's whereabouts nailed down. That way Jake and Marcus can hit the ground running and work out a plan."

"Yes, ma'am."

"Now, let's get airborne."

———

Pakistan

The fields were crisscrossed with drainage ditches which reminded Hawk of the ones he'd crawled through before in Afghanistan. Every so often a tree punctuated the flat landscape but mostly it was bare. A herd of goats ate lazily while their shepherd, a young boy, watched over them.

The sun was going down and the target compound was three-hundred meters away. In the twelve hours that they had been onsite, Hawk and Gray had identified the SAS OP and worked out how many X-rays were inside the compound itself. Now all they had to do was get in, neutralize the threat, and get out again with their package.

"Once the sun goes down, we move," Hawk said to Gray.

"You know they're going to see us, right," Gray said. "They've more than likely got eyes in the sky."

"Yes, but they don't have Slania. You find that signal yet?"

"Who do you think I am? Give me a couple of minutes and they will be blind."

A few minutes later, Slania came back over the comms. "Bravo One, your friends are in the blind. You're clear to move."

"Copy, Alpha Three. Bravo is moving."

The two Talon operators slid into the drainage ditch just as the sun was disappearing below the horizon to the west. Both men were armed with suppressed HK 416s and Glock handguns. Beneath their body armor and clothing they wore their Synoprathetic suits. They also wore ballistic helmets equipped with NVGs, their rifles having laser sights.

The water in the bottom of the drain smelled like shit. Stagnant, slime filled.

"Maybe we should have thought this through some more," Gray whispered.

They started working their way along the ditch through the muck, slowly, cautiously. The stench filled their nostrils as they progressed. A dog barked in the distance, a deep guttural sound.

"Hold position, Bravo One."

They both froze. At first there was nothing and then came the sound of the bells. The goats were on the move, and with them the shepherd.

The deep jangling grew closer, louder. The bleating grew in intensity, then they appeared twenty meters further along the ditch. Just shadows because of the darkness.

Hawk waited, unmoving. His 416 was ready to fire, just in case.

The goats noisily splashed across the ditch in what seemed to take an age. Then came the shepherd right behind them. Hawk could hear him talking to the animals.

Then they were gone.

His comms came alive. "Bravo One, clear to move."

They started once again and thirty minutes later, after slogging through the muck, they reached the compound.

Almost certain that the black ops team from the CIA couldn't see him, Hawk came out of the ditch and ran towards the wall. He pressed his back against the mud-built wall and listened.

Everything was quiet. "Come on over," he whispered into his comms.

Gray came out of the ditch and joined Hawk at the wall. Once there he crouched down and waited for Hawk to make his next move.

"Alpha Three, sitrep, over."

"We have eight inside the compound, Jake. Two sleeping in one room, another two by themselves. That will be Azhaan and one of the guards. Four sentries. I'll guide you onto them."

"Roger that. Ready when you are."

"Go over the wall there. It's all clear."

Hawk slung his weapon and climbed the mud wall, followed by Gray. "We're in."

"There should be a guard around the corner of the building to your right. ISR has him sitting on the ground. He hasn't moved for a while so he could be asleep."

Hawk left his 416 slung and drew his suppressed SIG. Being as quiet as he could, he crept over to the building, Gray following close behind.

He reached the building and walked along its exterior until he came to the corner. Then he leaned around, and through the green haze of his NVGs, saw the sleeping figure.

Hawk shot him twice and the guard never made a sound.

"X-ray down."

"Good work. You'll find the next guard thirty meters further on. Be careful with this one, Bravo, he's a little more mobile."

Hawk moved along through the compound until he came across the next guard. The man had stopped and was smoking a cigarette. One shot in the head was enough.

"The next one is in the far corner of the compound, Jake."

It took a further five minutes, but at the end of it, the two remaining guards were down. "Going into the house," Hawk said.

The door creaked as Hawk opened it and he prayed that it wouldn't be heard. He paused, and then stepped in.

"Jake, look out!"

Suddenly the door across the room burst open and a figure holding a weapon filled the opening. The 416 in Hawk's hands rattled and the figure cried out as 5.56 rounds found flesh.

The figure dropped, and as he went down, the AK that he held discharged into the wall with a deafening roar.

"Shit," Hawk hissed.

"The other one is moving, Jake."

The second door flew open and this time, Hawk had time. He fired his weapon and shot the man in the legs. He crumpled to the floor and Hawk rushed over to him, kicking the weapon away. Retrieving the flashlight from his pocket, he shined it in his face.

"Marcus, secure the other room. We've got our pigeon."

"Roger that."

"Alpha Three, is there any movement from our friends?"

"Only in place, Bravo One."

Hawk knelt beside the squirming man. "Right, mate, let's get this over with and I'll let the women look after you. Where is Lisa Bennett?"

The recognition was there. "I see you know the name."

Azhaan spat at him.

"That's not very nice." Hawk slapped him. "I know

172

you're in pain, mate, but if you keep that shit up, I'll fucking bury you."

Gray appeared. "Jake, there's lots of interesting stuff in this room."

"Can you bag it?"

"Yes."

"Then do it. Alpha Two, we need extract from target. We're bringing out intel."

"What about the package, Bravo One?" Ilse asked.

"The package is down. Non-ambulatory."

"Copy."

Hawk stared at Azhaan. "Last chance, my friend. Where is the girl?"

The terrorist spat on the dirt floor. "What if I don't tell you? Huh? You kill me?"

"Yeah, don't think I won't. Or maybe I'll leave you for the SAS team on overwatch."

"What SAS?"

"The ones that are after Farhadi."

The man's gaze flickered.

"Never play poker, asshole, you'll give it away every time. What's it going to be?"

"Get me out of here and I will tell you what you wish to know."

"How far out is the helo?" Hawk asked Ilse.

"Five mikes."

"Roger that," Hawk replied. He looked at Azhaan again. "You fuck me over, and you'll wish I killed you here."

In the distance he could hear the helicopter approaching.

———————

"I should have left the bastard for the black ops team," Hawk growled. "He's fucking useless."

"I gather you got nothing from him on the ride in?" Anja said.

"Have you ever heard the expression, 'As useless as tits on a bull'?"

Anja gave a wry smile. "No."

"Well, he's it, or he's lying through his teeth. Anyway, he's on his way to get checked out and patched up."

"What did you bag?"

"I'm not sure. Marcus said it was a treasure trove of stuff."

"Get cleaned up and rested. Leave the sifting to us. Good job out there."

Anja then went and found Ilse and Slania. They already had the bag emptied out and were going through its contents.

"Just like old times, Ilse," she observed.

The Talon intel officer sighed. "The challenge of the hunt."

Slania moved a laptop aside and started looking it over. A few minutes later she was into it. Meanwhile, Ilse was looking through some photos. "I wonder where this is?"

Anja took one of the photos. "A city somewhere?"

"Looks to be," Ilse replied as she looked through the others. Then she stopped. "It's London."

She handed another photo over. "This looks to be some kind of gentlemen's club."

Anja frowned. "I agree, it's London. Maybe Frank Fitzgerald can use this stuff."

"Oh shit," Ilse said, a hint of shock in her voice. "Do we have a picture of Lisa Bennett?"

"Here," Slania said, passing over a photo.

"No, that's not her."

"Let me have a look," Anja said.

The picture was of a woman wearing a hijab. "Wait."

Anja sifted through some other photos and pulled one up. "That is Kaaya Ismat."

"That makes it worse," Slania said. "I just found a recording of her on this computer ready to be released."

"What does it say?"

"Stuff about her father, her mother, and how they will be martyred forever by her actions. And that those responsible will pay the ultimate price for what they have done."

"Oh, shit...she's become a Black Widow."

"Get that information to Frank Fitzgerald at MI5," Anja said. "He needs to know what's happening. Meanwhile, we still have to find Lisa Bennett."

———

"I'VE GOT HER," Ilse said holding up a photo. "She's in Syria."

"What's she doing in Syria?" Anja asked, not expecting an answer.

"Looks like she's a war bride."

"Slania, anything about Farhadi's operations in Syria?"

"Give me a minute."

Ilse passed Anja the photo. It showed five women in total. Each one looked terrified. They were flanked by two men with large, dark beards.

"So, Farhadi reeled her in and cast her aside."

"What's happening?" Hawk asked as he entered the room.

Ilse brought him up to speed and showed him the photo. He said, "How do we know for sure that it's Lisa Bennett?"

"The one we have matches her company profile picture," Ilse replied.

"All right. What about one from her home?"

"No, we don't have one."

"Do we have one of Farhadi's wife?" Hawk asked.

"What are you thinking, Jake?" Anja asked.

"I'm thinking that the woman in the Syrian picture looks too old to be Lisa Bennett."

"I don't like where you're headed with this, Jake," Anja said.

Ilse gave him the photo of Farhadi's wife. He took one look and tossed it on the table. "I hate to say I told you so, but I bloody told you so."

"What?"

"Look at her wrist, where the sleeve has ridden up. She had a tattoo poking out. Not that they aren't allowed, but they aren't allowed. That there is Lisa Bennett. The other woman is Saba Farhadi. We need to get her out of Syria. If we get her, she will be able to help us with her old man."

Anja shook her head. "Some days I feel like we're going around in circles."

South Croydon, England

Lacey Fox took her Glock out of its holster and gently pushed the door open. A security guard lay dead on the floor in a pool of his own blood. "What happened to the Commandos who were here?" she asked Travis.

"They were taken off by order of the Home Secretary. Waste of resources."

"Good Christ. So they were replaced by plain clothes security guards on twelve-hour shifts."

"Something like that."

All of the security detail that watched over Kaaya Ismat was dead on the floor of various rooms. Lacey looked at Travis. "How the fuck does this happen?"

"It happens when people have no idea what goes on behind the scenes and screw up," he replied. "I'll give you one guess what the target is."

"She won't be on her own," Lacey said. "It took more than one person to do all this."

"Yes."

CHAPTER FIFTEEN

London, England

A CELL RANG and the man holding it answered, "Yes?"

"I want to speak to Kaaya."

He held the cell out. "It's for you."

"What do you want?" she snapped.

"Hi, Kaaya, it's Lacey Fox. You remember me?"

"I do."

"I'd like to know what you're thinking about now."

"What I'm thinking?" It was almost a screech. "I'm thinking I'd like a television news crew in here, that's what I'm thinking."

Outside on the street, Lacey looked around at the scrimmage of people. Police, tactical response, MI5 officers, and back beyond the ropes, no shortage of press. "Not going to happen, I'm afraid," she replied. "We can't send the public into danger like that."

"I told you what I want," she said and hung up.

Kaaya turned to Bennett. "Let's see if they'll give me what I want. Then I will execute you for the world to see. My father and my mother did nothing wrong."

"They were fucking terrorists," Bennett growled. "Just like you, you crazy bitch."

"You made me what I am. Akmal Farhadi gave me the opportunity to exact my revenge on the man who took them away from me."

Bennett snorted. "Another terrorist. The man who took my wife and daughter from me."

"And here you sit with no remorse," Kaaya said in disgust.

"The only remorse I have is that I won't have the chance to see that bastard die."

There was a flicker in her eye.

"You know what he is, don't you?"

"He is a means to an end," Kaaya said.

"Believe what you want."

"I will. Now we wait to see what they do next."

———————

TRAVIS AND LACEY felt their blood run cold when the SAS turned up. Once they were involved there was only one way for the situation to end. When Venables appeared, it was a certainty.

"Just when you thought things couldn't get any more fucked up," Lacey said in a low voice.

They watched on as the MI6 man waved his arms around, giving directions. The SAS shooters disappeared off the street and Travis said, "They're going to assault. They're not even waiting to assess the situation."

They walked over to Venables, and Lacey said, "What the hell are you doing?"

He looked disdainfully at them both and said, "Get out of here. This is mine now."

"Bullshit, this is MI5."

"Not since it was handed to me," he replied. "Now, piss off."

Travis stared at him. "You're going to assault without even assessing the situation."

"Bad guys in there, good guys out here. Situation assessed, now fuck off."

"This is all about covering your own ass, isn't it," Lacey said. "I'll bet my life that Bennett doesn't come out of this alive."

"Careful," Venables replied. "You might find that your life isn't worth that much."

The MI6 man walked away, and Travis reached for his cell. He dialed Fitzgerald. "Sir, we have a situation down here."

He went on to explain what was happening.

On the other end, Fitzgerald was seething. "How many people inside that building?"

"With hostages and hostage takers, around fifteen."

"Give me two minutes."

"I'm not sure we have that long."

Lacey looked around the crowd of responders. "Where did he go?"

"Follow me," Travis replied as they started looking for Venables.

Almost exactly two minutes later Travis's cell rang. He put it on speaker, so Lacey could hear. Fitzgerald said, "He's acting on his own. Stop him anyway you can. Do not let them storm that club, understood?"

"Yes, sir."

Lacey grabbed a police officer as he went past. "The officer who was with the SAS, have you seen him?"

The policeman pointed back over his shoulder. "He's back there near the incident truck."

They hurried further along and found the truck. Standing outside was Venables. He took one look at them and said, "Piss off, I'm busy."

Travis said, "You need to stand down."

"I don't think so, now go away. I'm in command of the

situation. I'm about to give the breach order and I don't need you distracting me."

"You have no authority here," Travis said. "So either stand down or we'll make you stand down."

"No. Team standby. On my count...three...two..."

BANG!

Venables dropped like a stone to the ground, dead with a bullet in his head. Travis turned and looked at Lacey and the gun in her hand.

"Situation defused."

Then came the explosion from within the club.

––––––

"WHAT HAPPENED?" asked Fitzgerald as he approached his two officers.

"Initial reports say that two of the terrorists inside had suicide vests on," Travis said as he watched the firemen hosing down another smoldering heap on the sidewalk.

"Why didn't we know this?" the MI5 boss asked.

"We were still getting on top of it," Travis replied. "Then Venables showed up."

"Downing Street is going to fucking love this. Not only did we get innocent civilians killed but an MP as well."

A man in a dark suit appeared behind them, an urgent expression on his face. "I've got something."

They followed him to the incident truck where he sat down at the computer. The screen was covered in lines which moved around a lot like those on a seismograph. "What are we looking at?" Fitzgerald asked.

"These are radio waves from just before the explosion. What you are seeing now is just the radio traffic from the responders. But if we jump forward to the time of the explosion we see this."

There was a noticeable spike in the waves.

"Is that what I think it is, Eddie?" Lacey asked.

"Yes, ma'am. The explosion was remotely detonated."

"Can you pinpoint where?"

"No, sir, but it had to have been close."

"Check every camera within a three-block radius. Find out where."

"Yes, sir."

Fitzgerald looked at his two people. "I want to know if Farhadi was in London or someone else, got it?"

"Yes, sir."

"Do it, now."

Syria

The rough gravel road bounced the battered Land Cruiser from side to side, throwing the occupants around violently. Gray looked across at Hawk and asked, "Would you like me to frigging drive?"

"Don't blame me, it's the road."

"You've got eyes, haven't you?" Gray asked, throwing his hands in the air.

"Shut up."

"Have you two finished?" Ilse asked.

"What's up, your royal loveliness?" Hawk asked in his best toff voice.

"ISR reveals that the target has a minimal number of X-rays onsite. Best point of ingress possibly from the east."

"Any indication as to where the target might be?"

"None as yet. Will need to assess when you arrive."

"Copy. Out."

They kept driving for the next hour before pulling off the road and circling around behind a ridgeline. Once there they stopped and climbed out. It took them a few minutes to kit up and then climb the ridge for a better advantage. Once there they hunkered down to observe the camp below.

It was a converted village. Small, compact, and rundown. Guards roamed between the buildings while women could be seen carrying water. "Look over there, one o'clock."

"Is that a training ground?" Gray asked.

"I think so."

Suddenly a man appeared from one of the buildings, striding purposefully across to another. He disappeared inside and a few minutes later reemerged dragging a woman by her hair, kicking and screaming.

Hawk focused on the pair with his binoculars. "Are you seeing this, Alpha Two?"

"I have it, Jake."

"Orders?"

"Remain hidden. Observe only."

Hawk wasn't happy with the orders. "Repeat."

"You heard her, Jake," Anja said. "Hold position. Wait until it's dark and then you go in."

"Roger that."

Ten minutes later, the sound of a gunshot reached up the slope and the man reappeared, this time dragging the woman's corpse. Hawk's eyes narrowed. "You're fucking mine."

The perpetrator left the body on the ground outside and then went back to the building he'd got the woman from and disappeared inside.

"Alpha One, are we just going to watch this?"

"Hold where you are, Jake."

The man emerged dragging another woman. "Anja?"

"Hold your position, Jake."

"Shit...fuck."

Another gunshot, another body.

The terrorist went back a third time. Repeated his actions and then it stopped.

"What the frigging hell was all that about?" Gray asked.

"Power, dominance, who fucking knows?"

The next few hours passed slowly, the bodies lying in the open a reminder of what had happened earlier in the day. About an hour before the sun went down, things changed. "Bravo, you have seven vehicles coming in from the west. Looks like you're about to have guests."

Hawk and Gray shifted their gazes and spotted the dust cloud. At its base was the first of the inbound vehicles. Looking through the binoculars, Hawk could make out the figures seated in the back of the tray behind the cab.

"This changes things," Hawk said into his comms.

"If you want to abort, Jake, just say the word," Anja said to him.

"Not yet, Alpha. We'll see how this plays out. Is the helo on standby?"

"It is but you can't rely on it. Ten mikes is a long time in the scheme of things."

The vehicles arrived at the camp and disgorged between twenty and thirty fighters. Enough to get the watchers' attention, but not as much as the two prisoners they took out of the rear of the third vehicle.

"Are they what I think they are?" Gray asked in disbelief.

"Uh, huh," Hawk grunted. "Why does it always have to be missionaries?"

"Alpha Two, copy?" Gray said into his comms.

"Copy, Bravo Two."

"Our new visitors brought a surprise with them. What appear to be two female missionaries. I would say both are in their fifties and are a little worse for wear."

"Copy, Bravo Two. Wait one."

They watched as the two missionaries were taken to

the same building where the three women had been taken from earlier in the day.

"Bravo Two, can confirm that two days ago two female missionaries were kidnapped from a refugee camp to the west. The abductors also killed the three doctors onsite."

"Do we know who these wankers are?"

"Negative."

"They're well-armed."

"Affirmative."

"Orders?"

"The mission is still Saba Farhadi," Anja said.

"What about the missionaries?"

"Negative."

"We can't just leave them," Hawk said.

"You can't fight off forty fighters either."

"Hold my beer. Out." Hawk looked at Gray. "Get everything out of your kit. Let's see what we can do."

———

THE FIRST GUARD died silently when a knife slipped between his ribs and punctured his heart. Hawk lowered him to the ground and laid him in the shadow of a vehicle. He then set up a claymore using a timer. Once that was done, Hawk changed position and worked towards a building where the terrorists were sleeping. There he set up another claymore. This one, however, was to be detonated manually.

"Marcus, where you at?"

"Just finished."

"All right, meet you at the target building."

A couple of minutes later, the two operators met at the prearranged spot near the building where the prisoners were being held. Hawk said, "Keep an eye out while I go inside."

Hawk eased the door open and slipped in through the

narrow opening. He flicked on his small flashlight and shone it around the room. "Ah, fuck it."

"Language, young man," a voice reprimanded him out of the darkness.

He shone the torch in the direction and the face of one of the missionaries came to life. "Sorry, sister," Hawk said. "But I wasn't expecting so many."

His gaze followed the beam around the room and he counted ten women. The torch stopped occasionally. "Saba Farhadi?"

"Here," a soft voice said, and Hawk moved the light back to the right.

"Step forward, please."

She came over and stood in front of him. The Brit ignored her for a moment and asked in a quiet voice, "We're here to get you out. We hadn't counted on all your friends, but we'll pull them out, too."

"Do you work for my husband?" she asked, sounding hopeful.

"No."

"I didn't think so."

"How long have you been here?"

She shook her head. "I do not know. Since Akmal took up with that other woman."

"Lisa Bennett?"

"Yes."

Christ, the poor cow doesn't know about her daughter.

Hawk said in a low voice, "All right, listen to me. I'm going to take you all out of here. You do what I say, when I say it, and this might just work. And no talking. Understood?"

They all nodded and said yes.

"What did I say? No bloody talking."

"Young man," said one of the missionaries. "I will not—"

"Sister, I'm sorry, but will you just shut up?"

Her mouth closed like a steel trap.

Hawk said, "Right, everyone line up single file."

They did as they were told and Hawk walked along the line and said, "Each of you grab the person in front and don't let go."

He waited until they were done and then grabbed Saba Farhadi and moved her to the front. "You follow me or my mate. Listen to everything I tell you. All right?"

"Yes," she answered nervously.

"Right, wait here."

Hawk walked over to the door and turned off the flashlight, dropping his NVGs into place. He opened the door and found Marcus where he'd left him. "You ready, Mucker?"

"How many?"

"Too fucking many. We'll take them out in single file."

"Farhadi's wife?"

"She'll be at the front of the line. The timer will go shortly. Once it does, make the rest go bang."

"Roger that."

Hawk went back to the door and poked his head back through. "All right, follow me."

The ten women exited the small building which had been their prison. Hawk started taking them from building to building, trying to keep them in the shadows as best he could.

"Bravo One, hold." Ilse's voice was calm.

"What's up?"

"You have an X-ray coming your way."

"Marcus."

"On it."

Gray let his 416 drop and hang by its strap. He took out his suppressed handgun and moved forward. He edged around the corner of the building and saw the guard coming their way. He waited for a few heartbeats and then fired.

The guard dropped to the ground and Gray hurried over and dragged the corpse back into the shadows.

"Jake, all clear."

They started across the open ground to the next building when the first of the timers went off. "Jesus Christ it was fucking early," Hawk snarled.

"Language—"

"Shut up, Sister. Not bloody now."

A second timer went off and suddenly the camp was alive. Gray shouted, "Ideas, Jake?"

"Yeah, start bloody running." Hawk turned to the women. "To the building—move!"

They shuffled off in their line towards the building in front of them. Gray was down on a knee, picking off a newly appeared target. "Jake, keep moving. I've got this."

Gray grabbed his trigger for the claymores and squeezed. Multiple explosions lit the night, punctuated by cries of pain. Hawk followed the women, shooting at figures as he went. More explosions erupted, illuminating the darkness.

He stopped near the women and pointed at the ridge in the moonlit darkness. "Right, you all run towards that thing like your asses were on fire. Got it?"

"And don't fucking stop."

Hawk grinned. "Amen, Sister. Now, go."

They broke free of the cover and started their uncoordinated journey towards the distant ridge. A shout drew Hawk's attention and he turned to see three terrorists running towards the retreating women. He brought up his 416 and opened fire. Two of the three shooters dropped as they ran, face first in the dirt. The third guy kept running. Hawk turned to face them, sidestepping towards the ridge, keeping up a steady rate of fire. Bullets found their target and the third terrorist died a few meters farther away from his friends.

Hawk glanced over his shoulder and saw Gray coming towards him. "You all right, Mucker?"

"Still upright and in the fight."

"Alpha Two, copy?"

"Copy, Bravo One."

"We could really use that extract about now."

"I need a number, Jake."

"Two plus ten, over."

"Say again?"

"Two plus ten."

"Good thing I ordered up a truck then—"

Her voice was cut off as a Chinook blasted low overhead.

"You're a lovely lass," Hawk said into his comms.

"Just get to the LZ. You've got X-rays coming up behind you."

"Roger that." Hawk turned to Gray. "Get those bloody women before they run to London, will you."

Hawk turned and looked at more terrorists emerging from the gloom. "Shit."

He brought up the 416 once again and squeezed the trigger. The weapon fired twice and then stopped.

Empty.

He dropped the HK and let it hang by its strap. Hawk drew his handgun and walked towards his targets, firing as he went. Terrorists fell while others fired back. Bullets cut through the air and Hawk felt one clip his clothing.

The next one to strike home put him down.

———

"OH, GOD NO," Gray grumbled as he saw Hawk go down. "Please be the suit. Jake, are you all right?"

"What the fuck do you think?" he groaned.

"Coming your way," Gray said and started towards the prone figure. Bullets were whacking into the ground around Hawk, and he tried to regain his feet. Gray fired at the closest threat and put him down before reaching for a fragmentation grenade.

The former para pulled the pin and threw it at the remaining threats. "Frag out!"

The explosion rocked the camp. Gray leaned down and dragged Hawk to his feet. "Come on, get your sorry ass up."

"The women."

"Should be at the LZ."

"All right, let's join them."

They began a shambling lope to where the helicopter had landed and were forced to take cover when a small group of terrorists appeared and opened fire. They pressed themselves against a mudbrick wall. Suddenly the net was lit up by transmissions from the helicopter.

"...*taking fire*..."

"...*get them in*..."

"...*abort, abort*..."

"...*go now*..."

"...*coming out*..."

The Chinook roared overhead, and the two Talon operators looked at each other. "There goes our ride," Gray said.

"Fuck. Alpha Two, what just happened?"

"Wait one, Bravo."

Bullets hammered into the mud wall where they were sheltering. "Don't have a minute. Marcus, break for the ridge. I'll cover you."

Gray broke cover while Hawk covered his progress. The former para reached the last building before the open landscape towards the ridge, then stopped to cover Hawk as he crossed.

Then a white 4X4 appeared with a heavy machine gun fixed in the back. From there, things went downhill.

The *chug-chug-chug* of the machine gun boomed over

the camp as heavy caliber rounds spewed out fistfuls of hardened mud from the walls.

"Alpha Two, we're pinned down."

"Roger that, I'm trying to get the helicopter to come back."

"Forget it, we're trying to get back to our wheels."

"Copy."

They were about to start running again when their world turned upside down. A large explosion enveloped the camp from the center, radiating outward. Hawk and Gray felt as though they'd been hit by an invisible hammer. They were thrust to the ground, air rushing from their lungs.

Hawk rolled onto his back, and just before darkness enveloped them both, he saw the mushroom cloud rising into the night.

Who the fuck dropped a bomb on us?

CHAPTER SIXTEEN

Ankara, Turkey

"WHAT JUST HAPPENED?" Ilse asked, staring at her screen.

No answer.

"Tell me what the fuck just happened!" she barked.

"It was an explosion," Slania said as her fingers furiously mashed keys on her keyboard.

"What caused it?"

Anja moved closer to Ilse, placing a hand on her shoulder. "Bravo One, copy?"

Nothing.

"Bravo Two, copy?"

Nothing.

Ilse said, "Slania, check the radar images for the time of the explosion."

"Are you thinking that it was a bomb of some sort?" Anja asked.

"Yes. Get me a look at the impact area."

Anja said, "Bravo, copy?"

"There," Ilse said. "The bomb hit the target building."

"But where did it come from?" Anja asked.

"Oh, shit," Slania said and brought up the feed on the big screen. "Get a look at this."

They were all staring at the ISR feed on the screen when they saw it. A familiar shape drifted through the shot. Anja shook her head and snarled, "Find out where that fucking UAV came from."

"Alpha, copy?"

"Bravo?"

"Alpha, copy?"

"Copy, Bravo."

"Alpha, copy?"

Their comms had gone down.

———

Syria

"Come on, Mucker, get up," Hawk said, trying to drag Gray to his feet. He didn't know how long he'd been out for, but it hadn't been long.

"What was that?" Gray asked.

"Someone dropped a bomb on us. Now our comms are shot."

"What about the X-rays?"

"Don't know. Let's get out of here while they're down."

Hawk looked around. Things that weren't burning seemed to be destroyed. They started towards the ridge where they had left the 4X4. Climbing the steep gradient, they finally reached the crest, stopping to look at the devastation behind them. "Someone wanted that place wiped out," Hawk said.

"And us with it," Gray added.

"Come on, let's get out of here. I see movement down there."

"On your six."

They reached the 4X4 they'd come in and climbed in. "Do you think there is enough fuel in it?" Gray asked.

"I guess we'll find out."

———

London

Lacey and Travis walked into Fitzgerald's office and sat down opposite him. "Tell me you have something. I've got Whitehall breathing down my neck wanting to know how the hell I let this happen."

Lacey took out a picture from the folder she was carrying. "This is the person we're looking for."

Fitzgerald picked up the photo and glanced back at his officers. "This is nothing. A picture of a person walking away."

Travis nodded. "Like that it's nothing. Coupled together with other statements it comes into its own. We're looking for a young woman, early to mid-twenties, dark hair."

"Could be any one of a million people."

"And it could be Lisa Bennett."

"Why would Lisa Bennett kill her own father?"

"Why do young British women fly thousands of miles to join a cause they know nothing about?" Lacey said. "Because she has been radicalized."

"So, where do we go from here?"

"We've got everyone in law enforcement on the lookout for her."

"Fine, fine. I just heard from Anja Meyer at Talon. They just picked up Saba Farhadi in Syria. Along with numerous other hostages."

"Saba Farhadi was a hostage, sir?" Travis asked.

"It looks that way."

There was a knock at Fitzgerald's door and a fresh-faced young man entered. "Sir, I have something you might want to look at."

Fitzgerald got up from his desk and all three followed the young man back to his desk. On his computer screen was a picture. He clicked his mouse, and the picture became a feed from a camera. "This is footage from Barnsworth Field outside of London. If you keep watching, I'll speed it up."

The footage took on a life of its own and a Gulfstream appeared. A few moments later the footage was slowed, and a woman appeared and climbed aboard, disappearing into the cabin. Then she reappeared. The footage stopped and the young man said, "That is Lisa Bennett."

"So it is."

"It gets even more interesting from here."

The footage continued once again, and a man appeared.

"Is that Farhadi?"

"No, ma'am."

The man climbed the stairs and stopped. He turned back to look at something and the young man paused the feed.

"You've got to be fucking kidding," Lacey said in a low voice.

"Impossible," Travis agreed.

"I'm with you," said Fitzgerald. "But that there is none other than Michael Bennett MP."

"Then who is in the morgue?"

"I'm going to go out on a limb and say that it's Akmal Farhadi."

———

"LET'S PIECE THIS TOGETHER," Fitzgerald said as the three of them sat at the large conference table. "If that is Farhadi, how did this all happen? Don't hold back no matter how stupid you think it is. As they say, you can't get shot for trying."

"He put her on the inside to play the long game when her mother was killed," Lacey said.

"No, before that. It had to be. She was already working there."

"I'm starting to wish I hadn't shot Venables," Lacey said.

"What's done is done."

"Why would she do something that dangerous, though? Go undercover like that?" Travis asked. "There has to be a trigger."

Fitzgerald picked up the phone receiver. "Morris, come in here, please."

Moments later, Morris came into the room. "Sir?"

"Take a seat. I want you to dig into Lisa Bennett's past and find something that could be a trigger."

"Yes, sir."

"Right. Now, where are we at?"

Lacey said, "Sir, would it be prudent to say that Bennett used MI6 resources to go after Farhadi's cell and organization?"

"Yes."

"And the women that were placed with Warner that went into prostitution. What if that was him, too?"

"Keep going, Miss Fox."

"The thought was that Warner was doing that just to offload them. What if he was operating under instruction? The SAS team takes them off the street. They're used to get their fathers, and then given over to forced prostitution."

"Lacey might be onto something," Morris said.

"What have you got?" Travis asked.

"About six months before Lisa Bennett started with Farhadi, a friend of hers was kidnapped off the streets of London and somehow wound up in Syria as a terrorist bride. At the urging of Bennett, MI6 found her, and Venables got her out. She was badly affected by the experience. Raped, beaten. She was with them for three months. Only home a week before she took her own life."

"So it's all about revenge," Fitzgerald said.

"Yes, so it would seem. She must be good to have done what she did," Lacey said.

"I want DNA results on every corpse that comes out of the club. I want to know if Farhadi is one of those in there. If he is, then we can expect Bennett to disappear. His mission will be complete."

"No," Lacey said. "This is more complex than what we know. He lost his wife to a terror attack. He's going to keep going. He might have killed Farhadi but now he'll go after—"

"Muslim women," Fitzgerald said. "They see them as responsible for the death of Bennett's wife and Lisa's friend. It won't matter what country they come from, they'll take them wherever they can. Sell them, kill them, it won't matter. It'll be their own private war."

"Pass everything on to Talon," Fitzgerald said. "They need to know what we know."

———

Ankara, Turkey

Hawk stared at Saba Farhadi. She looked both scared and relieved at the same time. He thought for a moment before saying, "Your husband is dead. It was confirmed only a few minutes ago."

Her reaction was subdued, almost as if she was relieved that he was gone. "How did he die?"

"He was killed by Lisa Bennett and her father."

Saba frowned. "I don't understand. Why would she do that if she was with him?"

197

"Because according to MI5, it was all a plan. A ruse. Your husband ran a terror network in London." Hawk paused, waiting for her reaction. "But you already knew that, didn't you?"

"It is not my place to question what my husband does," she replied, looking down at her hands.

"But you still knew it."

"I had an idea."

"Why did he send you to Syria?" Hawk asked.

"To get me out of the way. He had grown tired of me, and the younger woman fulfilled his needs."

"Do you know about your daughter?"

"Guess I do now. One of your friends told me."

"We believe that it was an accident. The people responsible are dead."

"That will not bring my daughter back."

"No, it won't. I'm still sorry. A lot of people have died because of your husband."

"I know nothing of it."

"I think you know more than what you are telling. We will pass you on to MI6. They will ask you more questions."

"I understand. Tell me, are the other women okay?"

"Yes, they're on their way back to England. From there, the ones that come from Europe will be transferred."

"I am glad. Eventually we would have all been killed."

"Was that one of your husband's training camps?"

Saba nodded. "Yes, I think so."

Hawk stood up from the table and left the room. "I don't think she will tell us much."

"She probably doesn't know much," Anja replied.

"What do we do now?"

"We go back to Santorini and rest up for a few days."

"What about Bondarev?"

"We will get him. But first we need the intel, and the rest."

"Does Five have any idea where Bennett and his daughter have gone?"

Anja shook her head. "Not yet."

"Who is going after them if they're found?" Hawk asked.

Anja shrugged. "I don't know. I think that will be a Global decision."

———

Santorini

The villa looked great. Everything had been fixed and the bill paid. The carpenters and other trades had done amazing work to bring it back.

The team had been stood down for two weeks and were enjoying their time off. Regardless of them taking R & R, Anja had been keeping her finger on the pulse even while doing her own thing.

It was the first time in a long time that anyone had actually seen her having fun. It could have been lack of stress, or the gentleman she'd been keeping company with.

Ilse and Hawk on the other hand had been joined at the hip, exploring their new relationship which seemed to be developing just fine.

This day they were walking along a narrow, cobbled street with terraces on either side. The upper floors were living quarters above various cafes and stores. "Look at that one," Ilse said. "I like the vibrant colors."

The one she had pointed out was a sunny yellow. Directly across from it was a terracotta color. "Do you think they are competing for the brightest color?" Hawk asked.

She wrapped her arm tighter into his. "Maybe."

They had been out walking all morning and now the heat of the day was climbing. Although the narrow streets with their terraces did offer a certain amount of shade.

The good part about where they were was there were no vehicles. But plenty of foot traffic.

Ilse stopped and pulled out a chair from a small table. "Here, I'm hungry."

"All right," Hawk said, sitting down opposite her. "Café food it is."

Ilse ordered coffee and a Mediterranean salad. Hawk, something a little less recognizable, but with the coffee. They had been seated for twenty minutes when Hawk noticed a familiar face seated at a table two along from theirs. He said to Ilse, "I'll be right back."

"Where are you going?"

"To see an old friend."

She gave him a quizzical look. "What do you mean?"

"Wait here."

He walked over to the table and sat down. "Hello, Robbie."

"Jake, I was wondering if you'd notice me here."

"Bit hard when you're sticking out like dog's bollocks."

"Yeah, I guess so."

"What's the Regiment doing in Santorini?" Hawk asked.

"Not really with the Regiment anymore," Robbie said.

"I must say, I'm disappointed to hear that, Robbie."

"Yeah, well, the pay is much better now."

Hawk glanced at Ilse. She was still seated alone.

"She's fine, Jake. I'm on my own."

"I assume since you allowed me to see you, that there is a reason for this little visit?" Hawk asked.

Robbie nodded. "I owe you, Jake. I'm sticking my neck out giving you this warning, but I'm doing it anyway."

"Bounty hunters?" Hawk asked.

"No. I work for a woman. Well, a woman and her father."

"The Bennetts?"

"That's them. He was an MP. Now they're so dark they need NVGs just to see."

"He was kidnapping girls off the street, using them to kill their fathers, and then selling them to prostitution rings."

"All terrorists, Jake."

"No, Robbie, they weren't. Yes, some were, but not all."

"Collateral damage," Robbie said as though it was justified.

"Fuck off, Robbie. That's bullshit and you know it."

"I'm not here to argue right or wrong, Jake," Robbie said.

"Then what the fuck are you here for?"

"At this time one of your people is being picked up by the team I work with."

Hawk glanced at Ilse.

"No, not her."

"Be very careful about what you say, next, Robbie. They may be the last words you ever utter."

"They won't be harmed straight away, Jake. It is designed to draw your whole team in so they can all be rolled up together."

"Payback? Is that it, Robbie?"

"I guess so," the former Regiment man replied.

"Where and when?"

"I don't know. Like I said, I could be killed for telling you this. From what I've heard you have the resources to get whatever needs to be done, done."

Hawk stared at him, trying to read his mind. Then he saw his eyes flicker upward to the balcony across the street behind Hawk. Before the Talon operative could move,

Robbie's head snapped back, a hole appearing in his forehead.

"Shit," Hawk growled and threw himself sideways off the chair.

He rolled onto his back, drawing his Glock. The weapon came up and fired, bullets ricocheting off the balcony rail. Hawk cursed as the shooter disappeared, and he lunged to his feet. He looked at Ilse and shouted, "Find out where everyone is. They're after one of us."

"Jake—"

"Move, girl. I'll be fine."

He ran across the street to a doorway. He tried the handle, finding it unlocked. Hawk burst inside and ran up the internal stairs to the apartment above the street. He rammed his way in and found the owner unconscious on the floor.

A door slammed above, and Hawk ran back out into the stairwell. He ran up the stairs and through the door which led onto the rooftop. Hawk jumped back as a bullet cracked close to his head.

The Brit opened fire with his Glock at a figure retreating across the rooftop. He watched as the man leaped across a gap between buildings and kept going.

"This is bullshit," Hawk snapped and started to follow.

He hesitated at the gap the man had jumped, hissing a curse before backing up. Then with a runup far too short to make the distance, committed himself to the leap.

And fell short.

Pain shot through his body as he landed half on and half over the edge of the precipice. Hawk dragged himself up and winced as he straightened up. The man was still running but then suddenly disappeared downward.

"Why can't they just stand and shoot like normal bad guys," Hawk muttered and started running again.

He jumped a low whitewashed wall onto another

rooftop which was lined with washing. Navigating the obstacle, Hawk then leaped over another.

"Whoa!"

He stopped suddenly, preventing his plunge over the edge into a courtyard. Below him were three young ladies dressed in skimpy bikinis. They milled around looking confused. Hawk jumped down, startling them.

"Where did he go?"

"That way," one of the young women said, pointing towards a gateway.

Hawk smiled at her. "Australian?"

"You better believe it."

"Thanks."

"Don't forget to come back for a swim," she called after him, "Mister Bond."

The gateway led out into a narrow laneway which went up via some long, cobbled steps. Near the top, Hawk saw his target disappear around a corner.

"Bloody hell, I need a change of career."

The steps were hard to run up, for every time the Brit wanted to put a foot down, he had to short step or extend his stride.

At the top, he turned right and started along a laneway which doubled as a market street. Handbags, hats, and clothing all hung on walls out the front of small stores.

Ahead of Hawk, the killer weaved through locals and tourists then disappeared through a pair of brightly painted blue doors.

Hawk hit the doors hard, and they flew open. Another courtyard, this one empty apart from sun chairs and an umbrella.

And a man with a gun.

"Christ!" Hawk exclaimed and threw himself behind a chair all too aware that he had no Synoprathetic suit on beneath his clothes.

The killer fired and the bullet hit the chair Hawk was

hiding behind. Hawk rolled away from it, and lying on his back, opened fire.

The Glock roared twice, both rounds hammering into the shooter's chest. The killer rose onto his toes before teetering to the left and falling to the paved area with a sickening thud.

Hawk came to his feet, the weapon in his hand unwavering as it remained pointed at the prone figure.

The Brit checked him and found that he was most definitely dead. He then went through the man's pockets but found him clean. Hawk dug into his own pocket for his cell and dialed Ilse. "Talk to me."

"I was able to contact everyone, Jake. What's happening?"

"Before Robbie was killed, he warned me that one of the team was being taken."

"You knew him?"

"Yes, we were in the Regiment together. Now he's working for Michael and Lisa Bennett. Or was working."

Suddenly there were muffled sounds followed by raised voices, and then silence.

"Ilse?"

Nothing.

"Ilse, talk to me."

His demand was met by silence

"Shit, not again."

———

EVERYONE WAS BACK at the villa when he arrived, even Anja's new friend. "They've got Ilse," Hawk said. "Slania, time for you to work your magic, love."

She moved without hesitation. "I'm on it."

"Who has got who?" the man asked.

Hawk stared at him. "Who are you?"

"I'm Icarus."

"You what?"

"Jake, be nice," Anja cautioned him. "Icarus is a detective. He can help us."

"A detective. Can you shut down the whole of Santorini?"

"I can try."

"Then do it before they get her off the island."

"Who?" Anja asked.

"The Bennetts."

"They're here?"

"Their people are. They killed one of their own and I got the other," Hawk explained.

"Is that what she called about?" Anja asked.

"Yes."

"You killed someone?" Icarus asked.

"Have you got the island shut down yet?" Hawk demanded.

"Jake, take a breath. We'll find her," Anja said.

"Yeah, I hope you're right."

CHAPTER SEVENTEEN

Santorini

"THEY USED a sea plane to get her off the island," Slania said. "They had her in the air within thirty minutes of taking her. There was nothing we could do. Now we have to find where they took her."

"That's what they want," Hawk said. "It was their plan all along."

"All we have to do is find them."

"Any ideas?" Hawk asked her.

"I'm working on something."

"Care to share?"

"I ran traces through cameras and satellite and came up with Argentina," Slania said.

"Argentina?"

"Yes. My guess is that they've set up a place in the jungle somewhere out of the way. Bribed whoever they needed to and have a force of armed people to protect them."

"Then we need to go there," Hawk said.

"Just as soon as we know where. I'm still working on it,

Jake. And like you said, they're using her to get to us. They'll keep her alive."

"How do we find out if they're there for sure?" Hawk asked.

"We find the right person to ask," Slania said.

"Who might that be?"

"The person they bribed to allow them into the country."

"Who's that?"

"The Argentinian Ambassador in London," Slania replied.

"Shit."

"Don't worry, Anja is working on it."

London

"Just so there is no misunderstanding, you're asking me to kidnap the Argentine ambassador and interrogate him on the off chance that wanted fugitives are in his country and they might have one of your people? Am I right?"

"Yes, Frank," Anja said.

Fitzgerald sighed. "I just know this is going to blow up in my face."

"You'll do it?"

"Yes."

"Thank you, Frank."

"Can't have you coming to London and letting loose that field gun you use. The city would never recover."

"He has that effect. But he is effective."

"Leave it with me." His voice held a tone of resignation.

He disconnected and hit his intercom. "Morris, find Travis and Lacey. Tell them it's urgent."

"Yes, sir."

Ten minutes later, Lacey and Travis were in Fitzgerald's office. "You wanted us, sir?"

"Yes, I have a job for you both which will need precise planning and is at the top of the scale for deniability."

"When does it have to be done, sir?"

"As soon as possible. A life could well depend upon it," Fitzgerald explained.

"What do we have to do?" asked Lacey.

"Kidnap the Argentine ambassador."

Lacey and Travis looked at each other and nodded. "Just say the word, sir."

"Consider it said."

———

TRAVIS LOOKED at the black ops team which was assembled in the offsite briefing room with him and Lacey. All were former SAS who now were part of MI5's Special Missions Division.

There were six men all told. Five for the interdiction in two vehicles and the other to provide overwatch. Lacey would be the commander on the ground while Travis would oversee it all from the offsite ops room with the small tech team.

"OK, no one uses familiar weapons. I want AK-74s and only Russian spoken. Two of you can speak it fluently so you are the only ones who talk. Understood?"

They all nodded.

"Right, make it clean, and no one dies if we can help it."

They broke up after the briefing and went to their vehicles. Lacey rode in the lead vehicle with the team leader.

The interdiction site was on a street where the ambassador had to pass by an alley on his way to the theater. As luck would have it, his itinerary fell into the hands of MI5.

Once in position all they had to do was wait.

"We have movement from the embassy," Travis said over the comms to the team. "Target is five minutes out."

Lacey said, "Charlie Team, check in."

Each member called in one at a time except for those with her. The minutes seemed to drag by as though they were hours.

"Two mikes out, standby."

The team in Lacey's car checked their weapons and the driver started the motor.

"Team Two following, ready for interdiction."

"Team One standing by."

"Target one mike out."

Headlights came closer. "Charlie Two, we need a break in the traffic. It's too close," Lacey said.

"Charlie Two, roger."

The chase vehicle sped up and tapped the rear of the target vehicle causing it to slow.

"Go! Go! Go!" Lacey said and the vehicle she was in shot forward.

It stopped in front of the embassy vehicle causing the driver to stomp on the brakes, bringing the vehicle to a sudden stop. Doors flew open on the interdiction vehicles and the masked teams all climbed out, weapons ready.

Lacey stayed in the lead car while the teams did their work. She watched as Charlie One tried the door on the embassy vehicle. It was locked and the exterior armored. He reached into a pouch and slapped something against the rear passenger door. Then he backed off and waited.

Within moments there was an explosion and the door burst open. Then Charlie One threw a flashbang inside the car and stepped back once more.

The sound of the detonation was contained within the vehicle.

The Charlie One team members rushed forward and dragged the target from the vehicle. Half carrying him, they brought him across to their intercept vehicle and then bundled him into the back. For the moment, both vehicles were speeding away. The whole operation had taken less than 3 minutes.

Over her comms Lacey heard Travis say, "Operation complete. Return to nest."

———

LACEY AND TRAVIS stared at the Argentine ambassador, who sat across the table from them. The man looked afraid. Uncertain as to what was happening. Since his arrival, no one had spoken to him. He had been placed in a seat and handcuffed him to the steel bar that ran across in front of him.

"What do you want from me?" he asked, looking around at the team.

They just stared at him in silence.

"I asked you a question. This is highly illegal. I am the ambassador to Argentina. You will go to prison for this."

"You will answer our questions," Travis said.

"You are British? I have been kidnapped by the British?"

"Just shut the fuck up and listen," Lacey said.

"I will not be spoken to like this," he blustered, his face turning red.

"You will be. I will fucking kill you. Bury you in a deep, dark hole where you'll never be found. Do you understand?"

The man nodded.

"Not so long ago, you helped two people get out of the country and into your own."

"I do not know what you're talking about."

"Come on, Francisco, you know that's bullshit," Lacey said.

"I will not be spoken to like this."

Travis slammed the palm of his hand down on the table, his eyes burning fire. "We are not going to put up with this bullshit from you, Francisco. You will listen, you will answer the questions, and if you are lucky, we will let you go. But at this point in time, all you've done is whine and helped wanted fugitives escape."

The ambassador sat there quietly, staring at them.

"Now let's get on to the subject of Michael and Lisa Bennett. You helped them get into Argentina. We want to know where."

"I told you I do not know what you are talking about."

"Would you like to see your family again?" Lacey asked.

"What do you mean?"

"We have people watching them. One word, and they disappear."

"You are bluffing."

"Come on, Francisco, you know how this works. We do something, you do something, we do something. Then it all comes back to you answering the questions that we originally asked of you. So cut through the bullshit and let's get to it."

"All right, I helped them get into the country."

"Where?" Travis asked.

"There is a small village in the jungle to the north. At one point, there were rebels in my country who used it. That is where they are, them and their small army."

"How many people?"

"I do not know." The ambassador shook his head to prove his ignorance on the topic.

"I'm going to get a map. You will show me exactly where it is." Travis used his forceful tone to remind the Argentinian who was in control.

Francisco nodded and said nothing.

———

"They are in the northern part of Argentina," Anja said. "It is an old rebel forces camp. You will insert into the jungle. We will locate our HQ somewhere close by. Maybe in Paraguay."

"What kind of support are we going to have?" Hawk asked.

"None. You'll be on your own so take as much as you can. All we can provide is comms link and satellite ISR."

"We can get by with that," Hawk said. "Just get us on the ground. All we have to worry about after that is getting out."

"I have satellite pictures that suggest there is a helicopter onsite which might be of use."

Hawk and Marcus looked at each other. Then Hawk said, "No use to us, we can't fly it."

"I can," Slania informed them.

"That would leave the boss on her own."

"I'm a big girl," Anja replied. "I'll set up at the British Embassy. I'm sure they can spare a tech to help out."

"This may be a bullshit question, but you can parachute, right?" Hawk asked Slania.

She didn't take offence for it was an honest question and as mission commander, he needed to know. "I can do it."

"Great."

"Work up a plan, Jake," Anja said. "We leave in twelve hours. I'm sure you don't need to be told to have a plan B ready to go in case the helicopter doesn't work out."

"Yes, boss."

Slania said, "I'll organize the maps and photos. Meet you in the games room in five."

"Roger that."

While the others disappeared, Hawk remained

behind with Anja. He said, "This could be a one-way trip. You do realize that?"

Anja nodded. "I'm aware of that fact, yes. Do you have an idea?"

"Not one."

Five minutes later, Hawk, Slania, and Gray were hunched over a table, making out plans for an assault.

"We drop three kilometers to the north of the camp," Hawk said. "Any objections?"

Slania pointed at a spot on the map. "If we come in from the north it will mean that we have to climb this cliff at the back of it."

"They won't be expecting us to come from that way."

"I'm not against it," Slania said. "Just pointing out the issue it could prove to be."

"Marcus?" Hawk asked.

"Slania is right to point it out. But it could be worth the risk. Once we cross that stream, then we start climbing."

"No, it's no good," Slania said.

"All right, I'm listening."

"We need to set up an OP here on the high ground." She pointed at another spot on the map. "Because of the jungle cover, we can't pinpoint where Ilse is being held. We need at least a full day to ascertain her position before going in. That means we drop here to the east."

"The jungle is thicker there," Gray pointed out.

"Yeah, but she's right again. We can't just blunder in there." Hawk looked at Slania. "All right, I'm listening."

Slania's eyes moved across the map. "Here is our drop zone."

"That's five klicks away."

"Yes, but the jungle is thinner. Less chance of someone getting hurt when we jump."

"All right. As long as we're in position before daylight."

"Yes."

Hawk looked at the map and photos thoughtfully. "When we go in, I'm going to put you on overwatch with a sniper rifle. Any objections?"

"Are you asking because I am a woman?" Slania asked.

"No, I'm telling you because if you get knocked, we're fucked because we can't fly a helicopter."

"Then I will do what you order me to."

"Fine, pick out something you like and take it with you. Also, take an assault weapon."

"Will do."

"Make a list of what you want and what you all need. We'll go from there."

———

Argentina

Subtropical Argentina was a bitch of a place. Bugs, heat, humidity. Ilse had hardly slept since she'd been in the country. She had no idea where in Argentina she was—in the north somewhere, but she knew trying to break out on her own was not a smart move. She knew the others would come for her—she just had to wait.

It was late afternoon, getting on towards evening and she was hungry. Ilse had not eaten a decent meal since she'd been taken. All they had given her was some fruit. Guava.

She sat on the edge of a veranda, underneath the awning of one of the many huts in the small village the Bennetts and their mercenaries used.

Ilse slapped at a bug on the back of her neck. She hissed a curse and looked up to see Lisa Bennett coming her way escorted by a single bodyguard. Lisa turned and spoke to her shadow and he stopped where he was and she continued walking.

"I'm not sure which is worse, the heat or the bugs," she said to Ilse.

"Take your pick."

Ilse noted the thin sheen of sweat on Lisa's pale skin as she sat down beside her. "We expected your friends to be here by now. It is a little disappointing."

"They will be here. That you can count on."

Lisa nodded. "Oh, I know they'll come. It's just the fucking waiting."

"You know you'll be found eventually," Ilse said to her. "Just because you're hiding in the jungle with your mercenary army doesn't mean that you'll get away with it all. Killing terrorists is one thing, but selling young women into slavery is something else entirely."

"They did a bad thing to my best friend," she hissed. "They got what they deserved."

"Really? Those girls were all innocent. None of them were part of their fathers' businesses."

"No one was fucking innocent."

"Doctor Kaaya Ismat was."

"She had plans of killing my father. If I hadn't intervened, then she would have."

"Because he killed her father. There was an investigation into him, and he was cleared. Christ, you people are fucked up."

"I don't think I want to talk to you anymore," Lisa said, standing up abruptly.

"I must say, what you did was very brave," Ilse said to her.

Lisa paused.

"Going undercover the way you did to bring down Farhadi and his network."

"What would you know about it?" Lisa asked brusquely.

"I used to work in German Intelligence. I know more than what you think."

Lisa's voice grew bitter. "Really? Have you ever slept with a man you despise? Have him slobber all over you, grunt like a pig when he humps you? And then when he's done try to wash him out of you until your twat hurts from the scrubbing?"

"No, but I've seen people die in front of me. Friends bleed to death with nothing to do but try and comfort them in their final moments. And I've taken more than one life when it was called for."

"What of it?" Lisa said and started to walk away.

Ilse said, "My people will come, and many will die. Maybe all of us, but blood will be spilled here and not many will survive. Make your peace, Lisa. You might well be one of those shedding the red stuff."

CHAPTER EIGHTEEN

Argentina

ALL THREE HIT their drop zones and were now preparing to move on the target. They readied their weapons and donned their NVGs. Hawk checked his map and said into his comms, "Alpha, this is Bravo One, copy?"

"Copy, Bravo One."

"Bravo is down and ready to move. Will check-in an hour from now. Out."

"Roger that, check-in, an hour from now. Out."

Hawk turned to the others. "Alright, let's move. Marcus, you're on point. I'll be rear security. Slania, I'm relying on you to keep linked to Marcus so we don't get lost."

After that they began moving in the direction of their target.

Their path took them along a valley floor thick with vegetation and leaf litter, and across a shallow, rocky stream. Once up the bank on the other side they changed position in the line with Gray dropping back to rear security and Slania running point.

The next part of the trail took them over a steep ridgeline then down into another valley at the foot of it. According to their map, they still had a good way to go before they reached their OP position.

With the weight of their bergans burdening them they pushed on, finally reaching their destination about an hour before dawn: a ledge above the camp from which they could watch and observe.

Hawk said, "Once we get done, both of you get some rest. I'll take first stint in the OP. I'll wake Slania in a couple of hours. Once we've all had a couple hours sleep, we'll extend the watches to three hours."

Hawk settled in under a camouflaged net with binoculars and kept watch over the camp. During that time, he heard a jaguar growl and move around their position. After the sun came up, he counted twenty mercenaries with three roving patrols of two. And as luck would have it, the helicopter was there.

Movement caught his eye and Hawk turned his head to the left to see what it was. *You have got to be shitting me.*

A Fer de Lance.

The Talon team leader froze, trying to control his breathing. The serpent slithered straight at him, its path undeviating. Hawk didn't mind snakes, just the things they could do to you. Things such as bleeding from the nose and gums, headaches, vomiting, intestinal bleeding, and one painful death.

It wasn't moving.

He felt the coolness of the snake as it slithered across his hand. It paused for a moment and looked at Hawk; its mean eyes seemed to be as big as saucers. Then it turned away and kept going.

Hawk let out a sigh and thought he'd rather stare down a rifle barrel any day.

The next movement he felt was Slania sliding in beside him. "Get some sleep. I got this."

"Keep an eye out for snakes."

She stared at him. "Snakes?"

"Yeah, big bastards with a shit load of poison."

"Great."

Hawk crawled out and left Slania to it. She woke him an hour later.

"We've found her."

Hawk rolled over and grabbed his 416. "Show me."

Back under the netting, Hawk took his binoculars and said, "Point her out."

"That one there. The hut to the left near the large tree." Her finger indicated the one in question.

Hawk brought the binoculars up to his eyes and looked in the direction Slania pointed out. He saw her seated on the porch. Just sitting, waiting, making herself visible because she knew they would be coming for her and would need to know where she was.

"Good girl," Hawk muttered. "All right, we'll keep an eye on what's happening and then tonight, we'll do what we have to do."

———

"HOLD POSITION, BRAVO ONE," Slania said. "Engaging target."

Twenty meters from where Hawk and Gray lay, two guards stood talking. He heard the first shot from the DSR-Precision DSR-1 sniper rifle which took down the first guard. And before his friend could react, a second shot came in and blew the back of his head off.

"X-rays down."

Hawk and Gray moved out into the open, grabbing both bodies and dragging them into cover. The last thing they needed was someone stumbling across their dead compatriots before the team had Ilse.

Once the corpses were hidden, Hawk said, "Marcus, let's get Her Ladyship."

They moved silently through the village from hut to hut, methodically keeping to the shadows.

"Hold, Bravo One."

They each dropped to a knee and waited. Two more guards appeared. Hawk and Gray brought their weapons up and set their laser sights up to the guards' chests. "Execute," Hawk said, and they both fired.

The two guards dropped to the ground, making minimal sound. Once again, they dragged them into the shadows and moved along.

"Bravo One, something isn't right. I can see heavy activity near the building they're using as the barracks," Slania said.

"Roger. Keep an eye on them." He looked at Marcus. "We need to get moving, mate, before the shit hits the fan."

"Roger that."

"Bravo One, I've got five, repeat five X-rays headed your direction. Something is definitely wrong. The whole camp is starting to wake up."

Hawk muttered a curse under his breath. What had they overlooked? "Marcus, hold. We need to get rid of these inbound X-rays."

They took cover behind a small building and while they waited, did a tactical reload. Once prepared, Hawk said, "Where are they, Three?"

"They'll be on top of you in three...two...one..."

Then the group of shooters appeared.

Hawk and Gray opened fire and put four of them down. The fifth died with a .308 round through his skull from Slania.

"Moving," Hawk said as he started towards the hut where Ilse was.

He climbed onto the small porch and stopped at the doorway. "Ilse, you there?"

Almost immediately the door exploded in a storm of wooden splinters and bullets punched through it. Hawk dived away from the deadly squall and hit the porch floor heavily.

Hawk grabbed a stun grenade and pulled the pin. He slithered across the porch and threw it through the door where a plank used to be.

The grenade detonated with a loud bang and Hawk came to his feet. He burst through the door and saw a shooter staggering around. It wasn't Ilse, of that, he was sure.

He shot the figure twice and swept the interior of the hut. Ilse wasn't there. Somehow, while under observation by the team, they'd got her out. But how?

"Marcus, she's not here."

Gray backed in through the doorway, keeping his weapon trained outward. "How could she not be here?"

"I don't know."

"Bravo, you've got more X-rays coming your way."

"Weapons free, Bravo Three. Keep them off our backs for the moment."

"Roger."

"Marcus, set up a claymore."

"On it."

Hawk lifted his NVGs and turned on his flashlight. "Now where the hell did you go?"

It took him two minutes to work it out. Finding the trap door under the dead shooter, he lifted it and saw the tunnel beneath. "Marcus, we've got a tunnel. Set the surprise and let's get underground."

"Moving."

"Bravo Three, let them come."

"That's good, because they're on their way."

"Work your way down to the helicopter."

"Roger that."

Hawk dropped his NVGs back into place and went down the tunnel first. It was long and narrow, allowing just sufficient room for a man to stand in it. The Brit advanced with the 416 up at his shoulder.

A figure appeared and the weapon rattled to life. The figure slumped to the tunnel floor. Hawk pressed on, stepping over the form on the floor and turning the corner in the tunnel.

The sound of a blast shook the tunnel and Hawk realized that the claymore had been triggered.

Dust fell from the tunnel roof and coated the Brit in a thin layer. Still, he continued doggedly, Gray behind him now. The former para said, "I'd like to know where we're going."

When they reached the end, they found another ladder.

Hawk left his 416 hanging by its strap and drew his Glock. He slowly climbed the ladder and eased the trap door open. When he was sure there was no one there he opened it all the way.

The room in the hut was empty, though this one seemed larger than the other. Gray joined him and he walked over to the door and opened it a crack to see out. "Lights are on, mate, and they're searching for us."

"Bravo Three, copy?"

"Copy Bravo."

"What's the situation with the helo?"

"It's under heavy guard."

"Are you able to hunker in place where you are?"

"Affirmative."

"All right, hold position."

"Roger that."

"Jake!"

Hawk froze. "Where did that come from?"

"Jake, get out of here," the tinny voice said again.

"Speaker on the wall," Gray said.

"Can you hear me, girl?"

"Jake, get out, they're coming."

"She can't hear us."

"Camera on the wall."

"Shit. Alpha One, copy?"

"I copy, Bravo One," Anja replied.

"The package has been moved and we've got X-rays closing in on us. I need a location, now."

"You don't want much, Jake. Leave it with me."

"Come on, Marcus, let's get out of here."

"Bravo One, sitrep."

"We're pulling back, Bravo Three. The package has been moved somehow."

"Jake, I've got a vehicle leaving the camp on the east side," Anja said. "Ilse could be in it."

Hawk thought for a moment. "No, it's a ruse. She's still here."

Back in ops, Anja gave an order to scan for a hut with one, possibly two heat signatures in it.

Hawk and Gray came out of the hut and were fired upon. They both went to their knees and returned the incoming fire with rounds of their own. Gray took a fragmentation grenade and pulled the pin. "Frag out!"

The grenade bounced towards a couple of mercenaries before exploding. Shards from the grenade cut a lethal path through them, silencing their shooting.

The two Talon operators were about to move when Anja said, "I think I've found her. There is a building to the northwest of your position with two people inside. Neither has moved."

"Copy, Alpha One, we're moving now."

"Be careful."

"Bravo Three is moving to that position."

"Watch your ass, Slania," Hawk said into his comms.

"Someone has to," she replied.

The two Talon men started to push forward, killing as they went. Bullets and grenades cleared a path as more of the mercenaries closed in on their position. Suddenly, just as it seemed they would be overwhelmed by superior numbers, Slania appeared on their flank and threw a grenade.

That broke up the assault and the mercenaries disappeared into the jungle, beaten, demoralized. That left Ilse and whoever else was in the room with her.

Hawk eased the door to the hut open, once more preferring his Glock instead of his 416. The light was on inside and he saw them both. Ilse and Bennett were standing next to what looked to be a radio of sorts.

Bennett had a handgun pointed at Ilse's head. "That's far enough," he snapped.

"It's over, Bennett," Hawk said.

"It's over when I say so."

"Are you alright?" he asked Ilse.

"Been better."

"Where's your daughter, Bennett?" Hawk asked.

"She has gone. She will carry on the work that I started."

Hawk nodded. "What do we do now?" he asked the former MP.

"I guess that is—"

BANG!

Bennett's head snapped back, and he crumpled to the floor. Ilse stiffened and then stared at Hawk who was putting his Glock away.

"What the fuck was that?" she asked him.

"You're welcome," Hawk said with a cheeky grin.

"You could have got me killed."

"Never would have happened."

"Asshole."

"Are you alright or not?" he asked.

"I'm fine."

224

"Where was Lisa going?"

"I don't know."

Hawk said, "Alpha One, we've secured our package. One target is down hard, the other is in the wind, over."

"Roger. How is Ilse, over?"

Hawk stared at her. "She's fine. We're moving to extract."

"Well done, Jake."

Hawk looked at Ilse. "You ready?"

"I hate you," she shot back at him.

"And I love you," he said back.

Her eyes widened. "Jake—"

"Shut up. I don't know what came over me. Let's move."

"Jake, stop."

But it was too late. He was out the door and moving towards the helicopter.

CHAPTER NINETEEN

Tarikistan DMZ, One Month Later

NOT MANY PEOPLE had heard of Tarikistan. It was a small country between the Russian Federation and Kazakhstan, no bigger than the southwest Pacific nation of Papua New Guinea. And even though it was a country in its own right, it had become a puppet state of Russia.

Which was part of the reason for Talon being there. The other part was because Lisa Bennett had finally resurfaced and was about to buy thirty female Russian political prisoners to resell to the European prostitution market.

The location of choice, the destroyed city of Tarak, roughly ten kilometers across the Russian border. The first city that had been taken when the armed forces had invaded. Now it was classed as the buffer zone where no one lived, and all the bad things happened.

It was a meeting ground for terrorists, arms dealers, and people traffickers. Ideal for Bondarev to conduct all his business.

Lisa Bennett and her people were already onsite. She had brought an entourage of six, all hired mercenaries.

Hawk and Gray were set up in a partially destroyed

apartment building three hundred meters from where the woman waited in her Range Rover. Her armed escort provided a perimeter around it while they waited.

"Bondarev is late," Hawk said into his comms. "Anything on ISR?"

"Nothing at the moment," Ilse said.

Above them an MQ-9 Reaper UAV circled, sending real-time feedback to the crib where the others had set up their mobile command center. This was an observation mission. Nothing more. They needed eyes on Lisa Bennett so they could track her movements. Engaging in a running firefight in the city was suicide, even with helicopter backup.

"You figure Bondarev himself might show up, Jake?" Gray asked.

"Nah, that prick will be sitting in his comfortable apartment in Moscow somewhere," Hawk replied.

Waiting patiently like those they watched, the team noticed four other vehicles on approach twenty minutes later.

"Bravo One, you've got inbound to your position. Four vehicles. This could be what you're waiting for."

"Roger, Alpha Two. We've got eyes on. Getting the listening device up and running."

Beside him, Gray opened the box they brought with them.

The four 4X4s came to a halt and the passengers got out. Hawk looked through his binoculars and let out a long slow breath. "You've got to be bloody shitting me."

———

"ABOUT BLOODY TIME," Lisa Bennett growled as the vehicles appeared. She wasn't worried that there were no transports; they had already arranged for that to go ahead once payment was made. This was about

227

meeting the seller and arranging for more shipments in the future.

The vehicles came to a stop and those within climbed out. The escort was armed with AK-12s. The final man to emerge had gray hair and wore a long coat.

Lisa had never met Bondarev before and was surprised when he suggested that he himself come instead of his associate.

She nodded. "Mister Bondarev."

"Please, call me Nikita. If we are going to be doing business, then we should be on a first name basis."

"All right, Nikita."

"Now, the arrangement was for thirty women, yes?"

"Yes. All Muslim."

He nodded. "I'm afraid that my supply was a little short. But I have substituted the shortfall with Ukrainian women."

"That wasn't the deal," Lisa snapped.

"It is now. Take it or leave it."

Lisa felt the anger churn in her stomach.

"And before you try something silly, I might point out that I have more men than you do."

She ignored the comment. "There are still thirty women?"

"Yes."

"They're at the pickup point?"

"Yes."

"Fine, then let's make the transfer."

She took out her encrypted cell and opened a banking link. Before long she passed it over to Bondarev. He put in the numbers and the money was transferred. Before he handed it back, she said, "Just hit the button that says clear, and all your details will be gone. That way you can be assured that nothing is stored."

The oligarch nodded and did as she said. Suddenly

the screen went weird and then black. He frowned. "I think your phone just shit itself."

"Not quite, it was your bank account. You see, my father taught me one thing—don't let anyone take advantage of you."

Then the mercenaries brought their weapons up and the killing began.

———

"OH, shit, we've got a situation here, Alpha Two," Hawk blurted out just before the shooting started.

Bondarev's men fell under the weight of gunfire from the well-trained mercenaries. They all dropped to the ground, felled by the deliberate shots which could only be taught at the elite level.

At first the conversation had seemed normal, Hawk even thought everything was going to go smoothly. The only thing they were missing was the location of the pickup. Then Bondarev changed the parameters of the deal—no great drama. Little did he know that Lisa Bennett had taken those parameters and thrown them out the window.

"Just sit tight, Jake, and we'll see what happens."

"Won't have to worry about that bounty anymore."

"You're forget one thing, Jake," Ilse said. "That bounty is still on your head until it's lifted. The only one who can do that it Bondarev."

"Yeah, well, he's fucked."

"Exactly."

"Got any good news?"

"No."

While they watched, the mercenaries checked the bodies and shot the wounded.

"Cold bitch."

Then they got into their vehicles and drove away.

"I need instructions, Alpha Two," Hawk said into his comms. "Do we let her go or do we intercept?"

"Let her go."

"Roger that."

Bucharest, Romania, One Week Later

"Buy you a drink, love?" the man asked as he sat on the bar stool beside her.

Lisa Bennett stared at him. "A Brit, how original."

"You are, too, by the sounds of it. If I'd known that, I wouldn't have sat here. I'd have stayed home in Manchester."

Lisa wore a tight black dress with a long split up the side. She was in Bucharest for two nights until her business transaction was completed. That business being the delivery of twenty women to a man named Andrei Fischer. She traveled with a small armed escort of three men. The rest were with the women at the ship in the Port of Constanta. But right at that moment, she was drinking alone in the bar of the hotel where she was staying.

The man got up to leave. "Sorry."

"No, stay."

"You sure?"

"Yes. What's your name?"

"Paul Cross. Yours?"

"Lisa."

"Can I have the pleasure of buying you a drink, Lisa?"

She smiled at him. "Of course."

"THE EAGLE HAS LANDED," said Ian Groves, former major in the British Special Boat Service, commander of

M Squadron, now commander of another elite force code-named ODIN after the Norse god of war. These people were Global Corporation's specialist extraction/kidnap team.

Groves was a big man with dark hair. The rest of his team consisted of Helen Smith, who was a former soldier with the Royal Anglian Regiment and his second in command, and Rose Holden, descendent of a British father and Asian mother from Hong Kong, who'd been MI6. Paul Cross, who currently sat alongside Lisa Bennett, another SBS recruit, and Evan 'Chuck' Norris formerly of The Rifles Regiment, rounded out the squad.

They had been called in by Mary Thurston at the request of Anja Meyer of Talon. It seemed that their help was required with a mission that called for two experienced teams.

While Groves and his team targeted Lisa Bennett, Talon was at the Port of Constanta docks where they were about to board a ship with armed mercenaries running security.

"It sounds like Paul is having a good time," Helen said with a smirk.

"It involves the fairer sex," Rose said to her. "He'd be in his element."

"Can he hear us talking through his comms?"

"I hope so."

Chuck Norris sat on the sofa listening to the banter between the two ODIN women. The plan was set and they had only to wait for the dominoes to fall into place to execute it. "You two sound like a couple of old hens at a women's meeting."

Rose smiled at him. "Feeling left out, Chuck?"

"Sad because Paul was picked for the important part and not him," Helen said.

Groves stood up and pulled on his jacket for the room

service uniform that he wore. Tucked inside it was his taser. Norris was dressed the same way.

Now all they had to do was wait.

CROSS LOOKED AT HIS WATCH. "Well, I hate to leave, but I must be up early in the morning to leave for Germany."

Lisa looked at him curiously. "You never told me what you did?"

"I'm a security specialist who advises banks on what they need to do to protect themselves."

"Really?"

"Yes, what do you do?"

"I'm director of a newly formed company. I move products across the globe."

"Bollocks," Cross growled. "What was I thinking when I tried to hit on you. A good thing I got caught out."

Lisa smiled at him. "I don't know, your night has turned out fine so far."

The ODIN operative nodded. "You're right there. The company has been wonderful."

"What floor are you on?"

"Seven."

"Really? Me, too." She finished her drink. "Walk me up?"

"Why not?"

The pair rose from their stools and Lisa smoothed her dress over her thighs before gathering her purse and heading from the hotel bistro into the lobby. Cross noticed the three men who got up behind them and started to follow, but said nothing.

They walked over to the elevators and Cross pressed the button. The doors slid open, and they both climbed in. The three bodyguards tried to join them, but Lisa held out her hand. They stopped and the door slid closed. She moved close to Cross and pressed her body against his. She leaned in close and whispered, "I have a big bed."

———————

"THEY'RE ON THEIR WAY," Rose said urgently.

Groves nodded. "Put the security feed on loop for this floor and let's go."

A few keystrokes and Rose said, "Done."

Norris grabbed the laundry cart while the two women carried luggage as though they were about to check out. Moving out into the hallway, they hurried along to the elevators.

Waiting for the car to arrive, they watched the numbers climb as the elevator rose towards their floor. Groves took out the taser and hid it behind his back.

When the elevator dinged, the doors slid open. The ODIN commander took one step forward and hit Lisa Bennett with 50,000 volts.

She cried out and collapsed into Cross's arms.

It took them thirty seconds to gag and bind her so when she awoke, she wouldn't be able to make a commotion. Then they loaded her into the laundry trolley and pushed it into the elevator.

Rose and Helen followed Groves, while Cross and Norris moved toward the stairs. Groves said, "Meet you at the van in five minutes. Go."

The doors slid closed, and the elevator began its steady descent. When it hit the lobby, the doors slid open and revealed the three bodyguards waiting to go up. Groves pushed the trolley past them while they stared at the two women in the short dresses holding hands, dragging cases behind them.

It was that easy.

Five minutes later, they had their package in the van, and were all ready to roll out.

Groves grabbed his satellite phone and called a preprogramed number.

"Anja Meyer."

"This is Groves. We've got your package secured. You're cleared to go."

"Thank you, Mister Groves. Your assistance was most valuable."

CHAPTER TWENTY

Port of Constanta

"JAKE, Marcus, you are cleared for insert," Anja said over their comms.

"Just so we're clear, boss, the intel still says they're in the front hold of the ship, correct?"

"Affirmative."

"Roger that. We're moving now."

Gray started the van and engaged first gear. He released the brake, and it moved forward, around the corner of the shipping container and onto the dock proper. In Hawk's lap was his suppressed Glock.

They pulled up at the bottom of the gangway, Hawk's window down. The first of the two guards stationed there walked towards him. He didn't get very far.

Hawk's suppressed Glock fired, and the man dropped. Hawk switched his aim and shot the second man.

They moved fluidly as they exited the van. Their aim was to secure the ship before securing the prisoners. If they did it the other way around there would be no way of getting the women off.

Running stealthily up the gangplank, they reached the

top and stepped onto the freighter's deck. Turning left, they began moving towards the bridge.

An armed guard patrolling the deck, appeared in front of Hawk. Hawk's Glock fired twice, dropping the guard to the deck plates, and as he went past, Hawk shot him again.

They entered the base of the bridge tower through a hatch and immediately started to climb. When they reached the bridge, it was clear so they turned to retrace their steps.

"Jake," said Ilse, "the deck below the wheelhouse is the captain's cabin."

They opened the hatch and entered the cabin, discovering the captain asleep. Hawk's hand clamped down over his mouth and he said, "Make a sound and I'll put a bullet in your head, mate."

They bound and gagged him, and for the next ten minutes they swept the ship from stern to bow. By the time they had finished, five guards had been put down and another six captured. The crew, they locked in their cabins.

From there they went to the forward hold...and found it empty.

***

HAWK SAT opposite Lisa Bennett and stared at her for a long time. She remained stone-faced, silent, trying to show him how tough she was.

"It won't work, you know," he said to her. "That whole tough exterior thing."

She said nothing.

"We can end this by you telling me where the women are."

Lisa stared at a point on the wall behind him.

"All your people on the ship are dead. Those who

aren't, are in Interpol's hands. We know about Tarikistan because we were there and saw it all."

Her eyes flickered.

"Once we're done with you, we'll hand you over to Interpol as well. If you want to help your cause, and get out of jail sometime before you die, then it would behoove you to help us."

Lisa's eyes moved and she stared at Hawk. "I have nothing to say."

"Do you think your father would want you to rot in prison for the rest of your life?"

"You know nothing about my father."

"Why don't you tell me about him?"

"He was a good man, a caring man. He cared more for the British people than its own government." Her words were bitter. "When Maria was taken, he was the only one who did anything."

"Maria was your friend?"

"Yes."

"Let's talk about her..."

———

THE CELL in Anja's pocket buzzed as she watched the interview from the other side of the two-way mirror. She took it out and looked at the screen. Pressing accept she said, "Harald? I'm a little busy right now, but—"

"Do you have an email account, Anja?"

She frowned. "Yes, why?"

"I'm going to send you something I think you need to see."

"Can it wait?"

"No. Give it to me, now."

———

HAWK WAS ABOUT to ask Lisa another question when Anja burst into the room. She slammed her cell on the table before grabbing Lisa Bennett by the hair and dragging her to her feet. Then, using her considerable strength, she slammed the British woman against the concrete wall and snarled, "Where is she, you fucking bitch?"

"Whoa, Boss, what the hell is going on?" Hawk demanded.

"The phone, Jake."

"What about it?"

"Just look at the fucking phone," Anja roared, keeping her snarling face up close to Bennett's. "Where is she?"

Hawk picked up the cell and stared at the screen. There was a picture of a woman, mid-twenties, blonde hair, blue eyes. "Who is she?"

"She worked for German intelligence. Two years ago, she disappeared in Russia. No one knew where she went or what had happened to her. Until now."

"Yes, but who is she?" Hawk asked again.

Without taking her eyes from Lisa's Anja said, "Marlene Roth."

"What is Marlene Roth to you?"

"She is my sister."

"Bollocks."

————————

Somewhere in North Yemen

The truck bounced over the holes in the dirt road, violently jerking the passengers in the back from side to side. Without a tarpaulin over the steel frame, the merciless sun beat down, dehydrating the occupants even further. Marlene wiped at her dry, dust-caked lips, opening the cracks in them and making them bleed once more.

The truck lurched again and the guard standing in the back with them swayed as he hung on to the overhead rail.

They had been driving through the desert for three days, its heat overwhelming. Her mind wandered from the dehydration. Her eyes closed and then snapped back open as a jet thundered low overhead with a loud BOOM!

Their guard said something she couldn't understand and then laughed. He shifted his gaze and then said something to one of the women closer to him. She didn't answer. He shoved at her with a hand and her head lolled to one side.

Dead? Fainted? Marlene couldn't tell. What she did know was that the woman was a British reporter who'd been accused of spying against the Russian regime and then locked away in one of their many political prisons. She had a husband and two children in Sheffield.

The guard poked at her again, then when he couldn't get a response, slapped her face.

Still nothing.

Then he grunted and grabbed her by the shirt, dragging her to the rear of the truck, eliciting shouts of protest and cries for mercy. He yelled something at them and then dropped the woman over the tailgate and onto the desert road.

Another jet passed low overhead, its booming roar almost deafening. Marlene leaned back and looked forward in the direction they were traveling.

At that time the truck crested a ridge, revealing the snaking convoy of other vehicles all headed in the same direction. The same destination.

In the distance she saw the blackened orange explosion resulting from the bomb that had been dropped on the devastated city before them. It rose into the air like a roiling mushroom.

Then she heard the staccato sound of the automatic gunfire.

Beside her a woman asked in a low, crackling voice, "Where are we going?"

Marlene turned her head and looked at her. "We are going to hell."

EPILOGUE

Constanta, Romania

THE FIVE OF them sat around the table looking at each other. "We are all agreed?" Anja asked.

The others nodded. Hawk said, "Damn right."

"I don't see that there is anything else we can do," Ilse replied. "Not if we want to find your sister."

"What if we don't get anything back?" Gray asked.

"That is a chance we have to take."

"I still think I can find her without risking anything," Slania said.

"This way gives us double the chance," Ilse said.

They had talked it over for the past two hours, each of the team giving their opinions on the matter until a decision was reached and agreed to.

Not all had been happy with it, but they would accept the decision of the group as final.

Anja stared at Slania. "Have you come up with anything new?"

"No, ma'am."

"Then we don't have a choice."

The door to the ops room opened and Mary Thurston

walked in. "It looks like I got here just in time to stop you from doing something stupid."

Anja glared accusatorially at her team, her eyes burning into them. Thurston said, "Don't blame them. No one ratted you out. It was the next obvious step to take, and I knew you would all do it. So I hopped on a plane and flew out here."

They all remained silent.

"I am right, aren't I? You were about to release Lisa Bennett?"

Anja said, "It was my doing, nobody else's."

"Then, as I said, it was lucky I came. For going off and doing something like releasing a wanted felon would be a criminal act. Possibly resulting in prison."

"Then you'd better lock us all up, General," Hawk said.

"I don't think so, Mister Hawk. You will all stand down and go back to Santorini. Do I make myself clear?"

They all glared at her in silence.

"I cannot hear you?"

"Whatever," Hawk said and climbed to his feet. "It's fucking bullshit, is what it is."

Then he stormed out of the room.

"Jake, wait," Ilse called after him.

"Let him go," Thurston said. "He'll calm down."

"We have a chance to get Anja's sister back for her and you want us to sit with our thumbs up our shitting asses," Ilse growled. "It's wrong."

Thurston nodded. "Anyone else got something to say?"

"No, they haven't," Anja replied before anyone else could speak. "There is a chain of command and they have been given their orders. Will there be anything else, General?"

"Not at this time."

"Then everyone is dismissed. Prepare to fly back to Santorini."

———

Lyon, France

The M7 in Lyon, France, ran along the Rhone River and at that time of night there was virtually no one around. The driver and passenger of the prisoner transfer truck checked their mirrors and noticed the delivery truck pull in behind them. They glanced at each other and kept on driving.

Orange lights from the streetlamps flashed across the windscreen like an external disco ball from the seventies.

The passenger grabbed for his weapon as the delivery truck pulled out from behind them and began to overtake. As it drew level they glanced at the vehicle and noticed there were two people in the front.

Then the driver pushed his foot down further and it pulled ahead of them.

"Whoa, shit!" the driver blurted out as the truck suddenly swerved and stopped in front of them.

The driver of the prisoner transport vehicle stood on the brakes and the tires chirped as it shuddered to a stop. Four people appeared from the truck in front, all armed with various weapons, walking towards the transport vehicle. The driver grabbed for his weapon but before he could do anything, his offsider pointed his at the man's head. "Just sit tight and it'll be over soon."

The driver froze and watched three of the people from the truck walk to the back. Inside the cab the passenger flicked a switch which allowed them access. The fourth opened the driver's door and dragged him clear of the vehicle.

Within moments he was bound and gagged and face down on the road.

A loud bang came from the rear of the transport and moments later the three masked figures reappeared with a prisoner in tow, a woman, showing the effects of the stun grenade, a hood over her head.

She was bundled into the back of the truck, three masked people joining her. The fourth figure climbed behind the wheel of the truck while the guard from the transport sat in the passenger's seat.

The driver removed his mask and looked at the other man. "That went smoothly, Boss."

Ian Groves nodded. "Yes, it did."

ABOUT THE AUTHOR

A relative newcomer to the world of writing, Brent Towns self-published his first book, a western, in 2015. *Last Stand in Sanctuary* took him two years to write. His first hardcover book, a Black Horse Western, was published the following year.

Since then, he has written 26 western stories, including some in collaboration with British western author, Ben Bridges.

Also, he has written the novelization to the upcoming 2019 movie from One-Eyed Horse Productions, titled, *Bill Tilghman and the Outlaws*. Not bad for an Australian author, he thinks.

Brent Towns has also scripted three Commando Comics with another two to come.

He says, "The obvious next step for me was to venture into the world of men's action/adventure/thriller stories. Thus, Team Reaper was born."

A country town in Queensland, Australia, is where Brent lives with his wife and son.

In the past, he worked as a seaweed factory worker, a knife-hand in an abattoir, mowed lawns and tidied gardens, worked in caravan parks, and worked in the hire industry. And now, as well as writing books, Brent is a home tutor for his son doing distance education.

Brent's love of reading used to take over his life, now it's writing that does that; often sitting up until the small hours, bashing away at his tortured keyboard where he loses himself in the world of fiction.